Prologue

"Hurry up, Bitch!" Misty yelled. "Shit, I'm coming!" Unique yelled back. "Well come on then!" Misty snapped back. They threw their shoes and purses in their cherry red Jag and hopped in, then sped off.

"How much did you get? I got $3200." Misty asked as she was trying to catch her breath. "I don't know I still have to count it. Here count it for me." Unique said as she was trying to catch her breath, also. "Ok, call Daddy while I count it." Misty said. Unique was not about to call Shorty until she knew exactly how much they had. "Hell naw, bitch you know we got to have the exact amount before we call him." She said. "It's $2700. So together we got $5900. I am ready to go home, take a shower, and smoke a fat one. I haven't hit like this in I don't know how long." Unique said excitedly. "Bitch, I'm used to this shit, but I like a trick to give it to me. It's whatever though as long as we got it. Call Daddy because I am ready to go in, too." Misty said.

"Daddy, we just hit for $5900. Misty got $3200 and I got $2700. Can we come in now?" Unique said. "Y'all get 11 more and make it an even 7000." He said then hung up.

Unique put the phone down and the look on her face said it all. "He said to get 11 more and then we can come in." She said in a disappointed voice. Misty didn't say anything for a few minutes. "I'm sick of these selfish ass niggaz!" Misty snapped. "Don't trip you will be ok once we smoke a blunt. 1100 ain't shit. We gon get that fast." Unique said. Misty was not having it. "Bitch you and that nigga got me fucked up. I can't even do it no mo. You take yo $2700 to dat nigga and I'm gon take my $3200 and do me. Drop me off in Gardena at my people's spot.

Chapter One

BACK TO THE BLOCK

At 5'7", 160 lbs., 36-24-36 every inch of Misty's body was where it was supposed to be. Her milk chocolate complexion was flawless and her hazel eyes seemed as if they could see straight through to your soul. Her hair was long, jet black, and always looked as if she had just gotten out of the shower, which gave her an exotic appeal. She could definitely get any man that she wanted.

Misty hadn't been back on the block since she was a kid, but she always knew where home was. Since she got in the game she felt ashamed to go back to the block. The last time she was there she was squaring off, boxing wit niggaz, and now she was wearing mini-skirts, stilettos, and hoeing. She did not know how everyone would react to her choice of lifestyle.

"You can let me out right here. And do not bring Shorty back over here Unique." She said sternly. "I'm not." Unique said as she was holding back tears. "I'm not playing Uniqe and these niggaz not gon be playin if you bring him over here." Misty warned her. "Misty are you sure that you want to do this? I am sure that he will let us come in if we push the issue." Unique pleaded. "Check this out. I don't know about you but I'm much more than a pimp could ever handle or appreciate. Hoeing is what I'm doing it is not who I am. So, you can keep paying yo Daddy and I'm gon do me. No love loss, but ma we were never the same."

On that note Misty got out of the car and walked down the street to her people's spot.

As she got closer she got the attention of about five or six niggaz that were standing around talking about half a block away. The closer she got the harder they looked and the more amused she was. She knew that they had no idea who she was from that distance.

"Damn, y'all niggaz look thirsty as fuck." She said in a playful way. "Aww, shit. That's Misty's ass." One of them said. After a few minutes of hugs and "where you been's" Giz said, "alright Cuzzo you gon have to go in and change out of that shit you got on and put on some sweats or something." Giz was always Misty's favorite.

She looked up to him growing up. "Cuzz I am a grown ass woman, a sexy one at that. I can wear what I want, but yeah you can shoot me some b-ball shorts and a wife beater so I can relax." Misty said.

After a long, hot shower she laid on the couch and drifted off for what seemed like hours. When she woke up she heard commotion coming from outside and her phone was going crazy from text and voicemails.

Ignoring the commotion from outside, because commotion on the block was normal, she grabbed her phone. She had 29 missed calls and 13 text. All of them were from Shorty and Unique except for three of them. Knowing what they were saying and not giving a fuck she deleted them and replied to the other ones, which were about money that she needed.

She thought that she heard her name coming from outside. She put on a pair of Giz tennis shoes that were sitting next to the couch. Thinking that he probably put them there for her anyway. And she was out the door.

She seen exactly what she did not want to see. A white Denali, on 24's was sitting in front of the house. "That dumb ass bitch brought him over here anyway." She said to herself. Shorty was standing next to the truck arguing with Giz and two other dudes from the block, named Buck and O-Dog. Unique was sitting in the passenger seat.

As soon as Unique seen Misty come out of the

door she jumped out and ran up to her. "I'm sorry

Misty. He made me." She cried. "Get the fuck outta my

face, weak ass bitch!" Misty hissed. At the same time,

palming Unique's face, and pushing her out of her way.

When Misty was mad or on a mission she was like a

Mack truck. Nothing could stop her.

She walked up just before Giz took things a step

further than arguing. "A Cuzz, I got this." Misty

interrupted. "Bitch, you betta have my mutha fuckin

money!" Shorty yelled. "Check this out nigga. That weak

ass bitch over there got your mutha fuckin money. The

money I got is the money that I made, and the money

that I'm keeping. You can keep sellin that played out ass

dream to dat bitch, and any other bitch who chooses to

buy it, but it won't be me. Now, I would appreciate it if

you got the fuck off my block before this situation turns into something a bit more tragic." Not giving Shorty a chance to respond Misty did an about face with a mean switch of her hips, and her hair flung and almost hit Shorty in the face.

"Cuzz, I need to go to the mall, the liquor store, and the weed spot, immediately. So, let me know when you are ready." Misty said and winked at Giz as she walked off, heading towards the front door.

"Bitch, I better not see you down nowhere!" Shorty yelled, as he was getting in his truck. That put Giz in super "go" mode. "Cuzz, on DragNet Gang, you or that bitch won't leave this mutha fuckin block, cuzz." Giz yelled back. But Shorty was already smashing off.

Giz had always been extremely protective over Misty. He didn't really understand what had just happened. All he knew was that if it came down to it he was ready to kill and to die for her at any moment, and Misty knew it, too.

"Cuzz, fuck that pussy ass nigga. He does not want it. Let's go because I have to get some things that I need. I am not worried about him." Misty said nonchalantly, trying to calm Giz down. "A Cuzzo, if you have any problems wit dat nigga let me know. You know I'll murk cuzz." Giz said. "I say we murk da nigga anyway, just because he disrespected the homegirl in front of us like that." Buck said "Hell yeah, cuzz if that nigga was bold enough to come over here then he gon try something if he see you anywhere." Giz said. "Fuck it then, let's get 'em then" O-Dog said.

"Naw, y'all calm down. Like I said, that nigga don't want it. I got better things to worry about. A Cuzz, how long will it be before you ready to go?" Misty said. "Shit, we can go right now. Y'all niggaz wanna roll?" Giz said. "Just me and you right now. I got some shit to talk to you about" Misty said. "Fasho, Cuzzo. Let's go then" Giz said.

Giz and Misty always had a strong bond. Giz was 3 ½ years older than her, and since they were kids he looked out for her. They weren't blood related, but their families grew up together for three generations, so they might as well have been blood relatives.

Giz was 5'5", light skinned, with jet black curly

hair, that he wore in braids. Despite his height he was a beast. He got the name Giz, short for Gizmoe, from the Gremlins movie because he was cute and as sweet as can be, normally. But when it was time to go he was a terrorist.

Giz was not quite sure how to take what had just taken place. This was his first time seeing her as an adult and was taken by surprise that she had been hoeing these last few years. To him she was the same little girl from the block that he taught how to fight. This was all too much for him to take in at once.

Throwing Misty the keys to the S500, he said, "You drive Cuzzo, and hit the first liquor sto' that you see. I need a mutha fuckin drank." Without saying a word Misty caught the keys. They both hopped in the car and neither of them said anything on the way to the store.

Misty knew that Giz did not like that she was a hoe, but she also knew that he wasn't going to judge her. Still she felt this feeling of nervousness and shame that she couldn't shake.

A drink would do them both some good. Leaving the liquor store Giz immediately cracked his brew and Misty poured out enough Rockstar so that she could fill the rest with Hennessey.

Chapter Two

SCRAP, HE MIGHT JUST HAVE WHAT I WANT; WE'LL SEE

Giz broke the silence. "Cuzzo, what the fuck was all that about and where the fuck you been for the past four years?" He said. "Man, that nigga just mad cuzz I don't want to fuck wit him no more and that weak ass bitch he got can't get no real dough without me. I bought that truck he drivin in two months, cashed out. He had that bitch for 2 years and was still makin payments on a Honda. That nigga is weak, just a typical pimp that ain't got a hood bone in his body. Fuck him." She said. "So you been hoeing all this time, and payin pimps? No disrespect Cuzzo, but that shit is stupid as fuck. You are way better than that." Giz said. "I already know Cuzz, but shit happens and it is what it is. As of right now I have to come up with a plan real fast. I got no whip, no spot, the clothes on my back and 3200 cash." Misty said. "I got two other whips, so you got that. You can stay at my spot, shit you can have my room, and we on our way to the mall. So, those three problems are solved. What I want to know is, are you going to keep hoeing or not?" After Giz asked that there was silence for a few minutes, then Misty turned up the radio.

In no time they were parking at the Crenshaw mall and getting out of the car. "I look like shit." Misty said as she was looking at her reflection inside of the tinted window. Giz looked at her from head to toe and said, "I like when you look like that." Misty paused and gave him a look that could kill and said, "Like that? You like when I look like shit." "Naw, man. Cuzzo, I didn't mean it like that. You don't look like shit. I mean in those kind of clothes. You look like the tomboy that I love." Giz said. "So you don't like me as a 'sexy woman'?" Misty said with a forced pouty face. Giz put his arm around her and said, "I love you no matter what, but that sexy shit is gon get a mutha fucka hurt."

Misty smiled, "I love you, too Cuzzo."

Misty had one of those bodies that everything looked good on so they were out of the mall in just under two hours, with what seemed like a whole new wardrobe to Giz.

"Now I need a laptop and some kush. Then we can go back to da house so I can get to work." Misty said. Giz didn't really know what she meant by get to work, but he could sure use a blunt.

"Ooh, there goes a pawn shop right there." Misty said as she cut some lady off, who was a pro at honking her horn. Twenty minutes later they were walking out of the pawnshop with a pretty decent computer. "Go to El Segundo and Vermont. The homie Scrappe got the trees." Giz said as they were getting back in the car.

When they pulled up they parked behind a silver 745, parked on the street, There was an Escalade in the driveway, and what looked like a lowrider that was covered up next to it. "This nigga can't be doing all this selling eighths. What else does he do?" Misty asked as they were walking up the driveway. Giz ignored her observation and rang the doorbell.

"What it does Cuzz?" Came from a slightly husky voice as the screen was opening. "Garr Garr, just coming to get an eighth of that good." Giz replied. "And who do we have here?" Scrappe's voice got a little smoother as he looked Misty up and down. "Chill out Scrappe, that's my lil cousin." Giz was obviously annoyed. "She don't look little to me, but ok." Scrappe said, but still eyeing Misty.

Scrappe was about 5'9" with a husky build. He kept his hair cut short and waved up. He was a chocolate brown complexion, with clean cut facial hair. And the clothes he wore gave the impression that he had one foot in the hood and the other in the bank.

Misty was peeping his whole style and she liked it. "Excuse me, your little cousin is a grown woman and the name is Misty. Can I please get that eighth so we can go? I have business to take care of." Misty said with attitude and sex appeal. "Damn, Lil Mama. Alright, let me get that for you. I don't usually deal with small quantities so I have to weigh it out. Would you like to have a drink while you wait?" Scrappe said.

Just as she thought. He did not get all of this dealing with eighths, he was a big boy. She figured she would do a little investigating. "No, thank you, but may I use your restroom, please? And while you're at it, I only have a note so can you grab some change?" Misty asked. "Feisty with manners. I like that. Right this way Lil Mama." Scrappe replied.

As Scrappe and Misty walked towards the back Giz sat down and put his face in his hands. He was very irritated by the flirting that was going on between Misty and Scrappe, but he knew that it would only make it worse if he said something. So he just left it alone.

The restroom was all the way in the back which

gave Misty the chance to see two of the three

bedrooms, and check out the décor of the house. So far

there was no sign of a woman, but he did have a little

girl. The décor was plain but strong. Everything was

black, silver, or mirror, no color. Definitely the work of a

man, she thought.

Damn, she wished that she was dressed, but

nevertheless, he was still interested. So, everything was

under control.

Before she left out of the restroom she got out a

hundred dollar bill and one of her business cards. She

made sure that the card was not visible to Giz. When

she got back to the front room Scrappe was just walking

back in. He handed her a nicely stuffed eighth and a fifty

dollar bill. She handed him the hundred with her card

tucked under it, and shot him a wink.

"Come on, Cuzz. Business here is done. For now." Misty said to Giz. "Aiight, Loco. I'm gon hit you up later. I got some shit to holla at you about." Giz said to Scrappe as they were walking out the door. "Aiight Cuzz, anytime night or day, you know what's up. And Lil Mama, you know where to find me." Scrappe said as he was closing the door.

As soon as he closed the door he looked down at Misty's hot pink card. There was a black silhouette of a woman on the right, and in the middle was a dollar sign, her name, and another dollar sign. In the left bottom corner her phone number and in the right bottom corner her email address. Not being a stranger to the game, one look at her card and Scrappe knew exactly what business Misty was in. So, he decided to do a little research of his own.

"Alright Cuzz, we gon stop at the liquor store because I need another Rockstar, some more Hen, and some swishers. And I am sure that you can use another brew. Then back to the house we go." Misty said as they got in the car. Giz was looking kind of bothered as he said, "Sounds like a plan, Cuzzo. Let's roll."

Chapter Three

TIME TO GET THIS MONEY

After they got to the house Misty fixed her drink and rolled two blunts. She gave one to Giz and took the other one in the room with her. When she walked out of the room about 30 minutes later she looked as if she had stepped right out of a magazine. She had on some skin tight, dark jeans, a white and gold backless shirt, gold strappy stilettos, a gold coach purse and a belt to match.

"A Cuzz, which car can I use? I gotta go get this money back that I spent today, plus some." She said as she walked out of the room putting her earrings on. "If you are going to go do what I think you are going to go do then I am coming, just in case you have any problem wit dat nigga." Giz said. "You, think I'm worried about that punk ass nigga? Cuzz, I got more gangsta in my pinkie finger than that nigga got in his whole body. I am grown and I do not need a babysitter. I been doing this shit for four years and he ain't the only pimp I have left and might not be the last. I got money to get and that is exactly what I'm gon do. And I'm gon do it without you babysitting me. Now, which car can I use?" Misty said with enough attitude to last a lifetime. "Yeah ok, I hear you big girl. You take the Benz, I'll be following you in the Monty. And since I am sure that this is going to be a long night stop back by Scrappe's so I can get my own green. I don't know why I didn't get it when we were over there." Giz said. Misty was just about to put up a fuss and throw a tantrum, but stopping by Scrappe's was right up her alley. She wanted him to see her dressed.

"You could have stayed in the car. I won't be long." Giz said as they were walking up the driveway. "I know but I have to go tinkle. Besides, I wanted him to see what I really look like." Misty said.

"Back so soon?" Scrappe said as he opened the door. "Yeah Cuzz, let me get another eighth." Giz was being short with his words. He did that when he was irritated. "And can I use your restroom again?" Misty interrupted. "Help yourself, you know where it is. I see you're ready for a night on the town." Scrappe replied. "Thank you, and yes I am." Misty said as she walked toward the back of the house, switching her hips a little harder than usual.

"A Giz, you going out with her tonight?" Scrappe asked in a low voice. "Yeah, why" Giz said. "Cuzz, she on the hot sheet. She got more than a few niggaz looking for her. Mostly pimps that pose little threat. Nevertheless they looking for her so G careful." Misty walked out. "I'll be right back wit dat. Y'all have a drink while you wait." Scrappe said as he walked towards the back. "No thank you. I'll be in the car waiting. I have some calls to make." Misty said as she walked out the door.

Even better Giz thought. Now he could get the rest of the info. When Scrappe came back he continued what he was saying. "Yeah Cuzz, she been pretty busy during the last year or so. So far four pimps said that she ran off with anywhere from two to ten racks. But, it seems to me that they all either fell in love with her, her money, or both. She better be careful." "Check, this out. That's my fam and if any of them niggaz got a problem wit her then they got a problem wit me and we can do dis. It's nothing, you already know." Giz said. "Garr Garr, Cuzz if you need me call me." Scrappe said. "Fa sho Cuzz. But how do you know all this, you just met her an hour ago." Giz said. Scrappe showed him the card. "She gave me this earlier. As soon as y'all left I ran her wrap sheet. It's a pimp thing, you wouldn't understand. As a matter of fact I ain't been out in a minute. Where y'all going?" Scrappe said. "That's some crazy shit. But, I don't know where we going. She wanted to go by herself........." As he was saying it he looked out of the window, the Benz was gone. Giz just dropped his head and shook it from side to side. "She gone?" Scrappe asked. "You already know she is. Fuck! She always been hard headed, gotta do shit her way. Where you think she might be going?" Giz said. "Definitely not the to the track dressed like that. She probably gon play it safe tonight. I wouldn't worry too much, though. She know what she's doing." Scrappe said.

"Money make me cum, m, m, money make me cum........." Misty was singing as she jumped on the 110 N on her way to Hollywood. "Thank God I shook him. I love my Cuzzo, but it would feel weird working knowing that he is watching." Misty said to herself. She switched the CD to Plies. Turned it all the way up and smashed to Hollywood.

She knew that she wasn't touching the track for at least another month, but she wanted to ride down. No one would recognize her in this car. There had to be at least a hundred hoes down. Misty hadn't seen it like this in a couple of years, so she couldn't help herself. She reasoned with herself as she parked and changed into her skirt, that she had "just in case". "If I am down longer than five minutes without catching, I will leave. And, I will stay close to the car just in case I have to leave fast." She told herself.

Within an hour and a half she managed to go on

five dates and make $750. "Ok, that was a great start.

Now, let me continue on with my night as planned."

Misty said to herself, as she made her way back to the

car. Just as she was getting into the car she seen a white

745 hit the corner. She immediately knew who it was,

and knew that she had to get the fuck out of there. It

was Y.T. and if he seen her, he was not going to be nice.

And he was one that she would not fight, she was going

to accept whatever he did.

Y.T. was one of the very few Pimps that Misty

had a genuine love and respect for. Which was the real

reason that she left him.

"Ok, let me get the fuck out of here." She said to

herself, as she started the car and smashed off. She

made that right on Sunset, went up past La Cienega, and

pulled into the Chevron. She freshened up, changed back into her jeans, redid her make-up, and bought some gum.

Back on her way, Misty went a little further up Sunset to the Standard. She pulled into valet, tipped the attendant $50, and whispered in his ear, "Keep it close in case I have to leave fast." She shot him a seductive wink and a smile and walked into the hotel. Even without the $50 he probably still would have done it, because Misty had a way with men. But she knew that tips went a long way in her business, so she didn't mind tipping well. In fact it was one of her rules.

Misty had only been in the Standard a few times, but never to catch tricks. She had only walked through straight to the elevators. But she made mental notes to herself about the clientele and the set up. She knew that it would be a good place to work. Tonight was as good a night as any to try it out. She sat at the bar and scoped her surroundings.

When the bartender approached her she smiled and said, "May I have a double shot of Remy, with a twist of lime, on the rocks." When the bartender came back with her drink he said, "That will be $30 even." Misty pulled out a hundred and said, "Charge me for one more and a bottle of Fiji water, and keep the change." Yielding a smile the bartender said, "Thank you, just let me know when you are ready for the next one." Misty returned the smile and said, "I will do. So, what is this crowd like?" The bartender who was tall, handsome, and kind of resembled Ricky Martin said,

"This place always has very upscale clientele." Putting an emphasis on very. "Just stay away from bald guys tonight." He winked. Misty took a sip of her drink, went in her purse, pulled out another twenty, sat it on the bar, winked back, and said, "I am going to sit by the pool for a while. I'll be back."

Misty had a gift for commanding the whole room's attention when she was there. But she was no longer worried about the whole room she already found her target, sitting at the other end of the bar. A middle aged guy wearing what looked like a Rolex, a white button down shirt, that Misty would have bet her life was an Armani, fitted jeans, also Armani, white ostrich shoes, that looked like they were worn no more than three or four times.

As she passed him to go to the pool she "accidently" dropped her phone and it went under his bar stool. "Excuse me, I am such a clutz." She said in a very naïve voice. "No, no, no, let me get that for you." The gentleman said as he was getting out of his seat. He bent down to pick up the phone and immediately noticed her freshly pedicured feet, in her strappy high heels. As he came up he could not help but notice the curves that her skin tight jeans accentuated. "What is that fragrance that you are wearing? And my God, your eyes are beautiful." He took the bait, now it was time to turn on the sex appeal for real. "Thank you for the gesture, and for the lovely compliment. As far as the fragrance, I'll give you a guess. It is as soft as my skin, but not as smooth to touch……" She winked and smiled.

"I am going to sit by the pool, if you would like to join me." Not waiting for an answer to her riddle or the invite, she turned and walked away with the grace of an angel.

She found a quiet little table by the pool, and he followed. "I took the liberty of ordering you another drink. And might I say that you have fine taste. May I ask your name?" He said. "Thank you again. The name is Misty, may I ask yours?" Misty said. "Misty, that is a very sensual name. I am Shawn, nice to meet you." He said. "Same here," Misty said. "Do you come here often?" She asked. "This is the only place I stay when I am in town. It is very modern, upbeat, and classy. And the women are always perfect. But, if I may say, you have to be the best, thus far." Shawn said, as he placed a hand on Misty's thigh. Misty looked down, raised a brow, and said, "I take it that you pick up women here often. So, tell me. Should I consider this my lucky night, or should I get up and run?" Shawn laughed, and said, "As much as I would love to see you run, I wouldn't opt for that. But, I have a better idea, let's go up to my room and finish this conversation." Misty gave him a discerning look and said, "If all we are going to do is finish the conversation then we can do that right here." Shawn winked, stood up, and said, "Trust me, you will be more than pleased. I only have about an hour, because I have an early morning. Follow me, and don't forget your drink."

Exactly an hour later Misty was back at the bar checking her phone, and contemplating her next move.

It was barely midnight and she had already made $1750.

She had five missed calls from Giz, and two missed calls from a number she didn't recognize, that she was sure was Scrappe. She sent Giz a text, letting him know that she was alright, and figured that she would call Scrappe on her way in, so that she could get some more weed.

Chapter Four

MONEY AND EMOTIONS DON'T MIX

"Say bitch, I see you still lookin good around here. You need to fuck around and come back home." Without turning around Misty immediately knew who was behind her. That voice made her melt every time that she heard it. "Y.T., I should have known that you seen me the way that you hit that corner." Misty said. "Yeah bitch, you did know. That's why you smashed off the way that you did. If you wouldn't have stopped you would have got away."

Misty waved her hand to signal the bartender. "Can I get one more, and get him one as well, with no ice or lime, please. Thank you." She handed him another hundred and said, "Keep the change, and don't forget the Fiji." "Yes, Ma'am." He said as he walked away.

"Damn bitch, you must be doing pretty good

around here. Who you fuckin wit now?" Y.T. said. "I was fuckin wit Shorty until this morning. I'm sick of paying selfish ass niggaz Y.T." Misty already knew that she set herself up when she said that. Y.T. had been one of the two pimps that treated her great. And the only one that didn't treat her like a hoe, unless it was work time. She and Y.T. had always been friends. The real reason that she left him was because she could not handle being in love with a pimp. As long as everything was about money she was the best bitch ever, but she knew that once her feelings got involved that she would change. She did not want him to see that side of her. He did not know that though.

"Bitch, I don't wanna hear it cuzz I was never selfish wit you. As a matter of fact, let me get the fuck outta here before I fuck you up for saying that shit to me." Y.T. had a look of pure disgust on his face. "You not gon break me?" She looked and sounded confused when she asked. "Naw, bitch. I don't need your money, and you know it. As a matter of fact, I don't want yo money no more than I want you. Faggot ass bitch." And he walked off.

"I love you Y.T. and I'm sorry for leaving you." Misty whispered to herself. She finished her drink, wave to the bartender, and walked toward the valet.

She handed the attendant her ticket and took a seat on the bench. "Hey, sexy. Where's the excitement tonight?" Misty looked up and seen a middle aged bald guy standing over her. She thanked God that the car was pulling up. "I have no idea, but I hope that you find it." She said dismissively as she got up, handed the attendant a twenty and got in the car.

As soon as she got into the car she checked her phone. She didn't have any missed call but she had a text from Giz, one from a trick, and two from that number she didn't recognize. She sent a quick "Be there in an hour to the trick," and "I love you, be home soon," to Giz. Reading the text, that she now knew was Scrappe, gave her a few different feelings. She was shocked, angered, turned on, and in a state of submission. Rather than respond to all of it or call him, she replied with a short, "Be there in 15 minutes."

She threw Trina in the deck and headed towards the freeway, speeding the whole way. It was 12:45, if she pushed it she could get her weed, give Scrappe a piece of her mind, get her money, and be at home, in

the bed by 3:00.

Chapter Five

When she pulled up in front of Scrappe's house

she got a nervous feeling that she was definitely not

used to. She wished that she had blunt rolled, but she didn't so she smoked a cigarette before she went in. When she walked up to the door it opened before she had a chance to ring the doorbell. "Have a seat." He said in a very stern tone. Misty immediately sat down, hearing the anger in his voice. "First, let me tell you that Giz has been my home boy for over 15 years, so I'm gon ride wit him over any of this pimp shit. And yes, I am a pimp, amongst other things. In case you haven't noticed. So, after you gave me your card I made a few calls and I found out how busy you have been and how many niggaz wanna fuck you up. Before you pulled your little disappearing act, I was letting Giz know what was up, since you obviously wasn't gon tell him shit. And it was damn there an act of God to stop him from riding down on every pimp in town to find out if they had a problem wit you. I do not think it's right and I do not appreciate you putting him in that situation, and if you was my bitch I would be whoopin yo ass right now and not talking."

Misty took a deep breath, trying to calm herself down. "I am going to say this as respectfully as I possibly can. First of all, I do not care how long you have known Giz, you do not know me, therefore this is none of your business. Second of all, I did not put him in any situation because I know how he is, which is why I left him here. Third of all, I am a grown ass woman, fully capable of taking care of myself. And not that it's any of your business, but when you ran my wrap sheet did it come up that the money I took was the money that I made the night I left and that those niggaz was either in love

or used to my money. I ain't worried about none of dem

niggaz cuzz when they see me they ain't gon do shit but

try to get me to go back and fuck wit 'em. And if any of

'em want problems then I keep the heat close by. Them

niggaz wasn't ready for me when they had me and they

for damn sure not ready for me now. That's they fuckin

problem and from what I can see yours too. I ain't no

hoe, hoeing is just what I do. While you running my

wrap sheet, you need to check my fuckin blood line and

see what type of bitch I really am. Now, can I please get

an eighth cuzz I got money waiting on me." Misty

reached in her pursed, grabbed a fifty, and held it out.

Visibly pissed, Scrappe stood up, walked over to Misty,

snatched the money out of her hand, and in one

motion, grabbed her by the throat, lifted her out of the chair that she was sitting in, and had her pinned to the wall that was about two feet behind her. "I will take that money and shove it down your mutha fuckin throat. You will never use that tone wit me again. I know who the fuck yo Mama and yo Daddy is, which next to Giz, is the only reason I haven't put you through this mutha fuckin wall. I don't give fuck how grown you are, your actions have repercussions. I will make this short. You will respect me, and you will respect Giz." He let her go. Catching her breath, and feeling defeated, she fell to the floor. He went to the back. When he returned Misty was fixing herself in the mirror and did not say a word. He sat the sack next to her purse and said, "For now on, let me know when and where you will be working. I understand why you don't want Giz involved, but someone needs to know where you are, just in case. Save my number in your phone and use it when you need or want to. You are welcomed here anytime, just call before you come. I am tired so I am about to get some sleep. Text me when you get in to let me know that you are safe." All Misty could bring herself to say was "Ok." Then she walked out of the door. It was not often that a man put his foot down and succeeded at his efforts, with Misty. Tonight two men had succeeded in breaking her down. All she wanted to do was take a hot shower and lay down.

She hoped that Ed would be quick tonight, and not want one of his marathon fuck sessions. She never knew until she counted the money on the dresser. She was relieved that she only counted two hundred on the dresser. "Oh good, I will be out of here in twenty minutes tops." She thought to herself.

When she got to the house she sat in the car and rolled a blunt. Her mind was bouncing back and forth from Y.T. to Scrappe. She could hear the hurt in Y.T.'s voice for the first time, and that felt like a knife twisting in her heart. And as far s Scraape, she was surprised at how she allowed herself to be treated by him, and even more surprised that she liked it.

When she walked into the room Giz was in the bed sleep. She grabbed the shorts and shirt that she wore earlier, some panties out of one of her bags, then went into the bathroom and took a long hot shower. About 45 minutes later she crawled into the bed with

Giz and lit her blunt. She felt bad because she didn't mean to worry him she just knew that he didn't understand the lifestyle that she chose.

"I didn't expect you until tomorrow some time." Giz said in a groggy voice. Misty leaned over, kissed him on the cheek, and said "I know. I love you, Cuzz." Then she passed him the blunt. "I love you, too. Always." Giz said. And they sat there in silence and smoked. That was all that they needed. He knew that she was safe and she knew that he would always be there. They both went to sleep peacefully.

Chapter Six

DADDY'S GIRL

"It's bright as fuck in here. What time is it?" Misty yelled as she woke up. "Too damn early for you to be yelling. I know that. Damn, let me close my mouth, I can taste my breath." Giz said. "Cuzz, I don't give a fuck. And it's only 8:27. I feel like I been sleep forever."

They both jumped out of the bed trying to beat one another to the bathroom. Misty jumped in the shower and Giz took a piss and brushed his teeth. "A Cuzzo, what you got planned for today and did you make what you needed to make last night?" Giz said. "I

sure did. I need to go see my Pops today and put some

things in perspective. Then, hopefully tonight will be

just like last night." Minus the mental and emotional

defeats, she thought to herself.

She jumped out of the shower and threw back

on the shorts and wife-beater. "I'm going to starbucks,

be right back." Misty announced. "Grab me a brew." Giz

yelled from the room. She thought it was kind of early

for beer, especially for Giz. But, fuck it, if I don't get one

he will just go get it himself, she thought to herself.

They sat in the living room, Misty on her laptop,

drinking her coffee, and smoking a cigarette. Giz was

drinking his beer and smoking a blunt. "You hittin' this?"

Giz asked. "Naw, it's too early for me, I have to get my

day started first. Plus, I don't like being high around my Pops. Misty said. "More for me." Giz said as he took a bigger hit.

"A Cuzz, what's up wit Scrappe?" Misty asked, because she could not stop thinking about last night. "He's a real nigga and a good dude, but he treats women like shit." Giz got straight to the point. "Like shit or like they want to be treated?" Misty probed. "Look, I don't know about or understand all of that pimp and hoe shit, so I don't know. Why you askin'? You wanna fuck wit' him?" Giz said in an unmistakingly irritated voice. "Maybe in the future, but not now. I got a mission to accomplish. He might be the type of nigga I would consider settling down with though." Misty said. "Well, I don't really know what to say. I am staying out of that shit. Just know that I always got your back, no matter what." Giz said, trying to dismiss the conversation. Misty closed her computer. Kissed Giz on the cheek and said, "that's why I love you." Then she went into the room and got dressed.

When she came out of the room she had on some green and white forces, light blue skinny jeans, a green and white v-neck shirt with lots of cleavage, a white Guess belt with a G for the buckle, a green starter hat with a white G on it, and some green contacts to set it all off. "How do I look?" She asked. "Like a true mutha fuckin GarrGyrl. That fit is nutty. You need to take a picture." Giz said with excitement.

"Thanks Cuzz, I knew you would like it. I'm about to go to da hood and fuck wit Pops. I'll be back in few hours." Misty said as she switched purses from the gold Coach to the white Guess. "Alright Cuzzo, G-safe. I'll be here. Tell Germ I said what's crackin." Giz said. "Will do, see you in a bit."

Misty was excited about going to see her dad. He was never the type of father that people approved of, but they had a bond that was unbreakable. He always kept everything real with her. Misty was his eldest child out of 6. He was 17 and her mother was 15 when she was born. Misty was always his pride and joy. She never held his street life against him, even though everyone else did. And the older she got the more like him she was.

As soon as she walked in the door she heard "Hey Honey!" That is what he always called her, and he had a huge smile on his face. He was always happy to see his baby, no matter what was going on. Misty could not think of one time that her dad did not greet her like that, and she loved it. It made her feel special.

"Hey Daddy, what cha doing? I got us something to sip on." Misty said as she tossed him a pack of cigs and went into the kitchen to fix their drinks. She mixed his with a third of water and hers with half rockstar. She handed him his drink and said, "Breakfast of champs." They both laughed. "Shit, I ain't doing nothing. Just watching Martin." He loved Martin. He watched reruns over and over and over again.

"That's cool. Daddy, I'm tired of being lonely." She just came right out with it. "Then get a boyfriend. It's simple." He said. Everything was simple to him. "It's not that simple Daddy." Misty whined. Under everything Misty was a spoiled brat that could not stand for things not to go her way. Which is why she always made sure things went her way with a nigga or without one. "It is that simple." He said. "Oh my gosh. Daddy, it's not. Listen, squares bore me, pimps are selfish, and gangstas are always gone. And my problem is that I want the life security that a square has, the dominance from a pimp, and the queen's pedal stool that a gangsta is going to put me on. And until I find that combination I am not settling down. The problem is that I am beginning to think that the nigga that possesses that combination has not been born and his momma is dead." Misty exclaimed. "You will find it Honey. You are only 22. You have a lot of living and learning to do.

When you are ready he will come. If he comes too early you might scare him off. But what I need you to do is stop breaking these niggaz hearts before I have to kill somebody." He said as he lit a cigarette.

Germ was about 5'10", with a medium build, black as night, with a bald head, and sleepy eyes. He was 39 but looked like he was about 25. He had a cold reputation in the streets as a gangsta, killer, and hustler. Most people either respected or feared him. Misty knew of his reputation and knew that he would not hesitate to kill any and everybody for, about, or over her. And neither would anybody from his hood. She was born on his hood day, which made her feel extra special. But thus far she had managed to handle her situations without having to call on any of them.

Misty sipped her drink. "Daddy, that is their problem. I don't be tellin' these niggaz to fall in love with me. And most of 'em just be in love with the things that I do, 'cause besides you and Giz, it's only two niggaz that know me to really love me anyways. Daddy, fuck these niggaz, they gon keep getting hurt until I find the one that I am searching for." Misty took a deep breath, sipped her drink, then lit a cigarette.

"You still got cha piece?" He asked. He realized that Misty didn't really want any advice, that she only needed to vent. And knowing that she was playing a dangerous game he needed to know that she was as prepared as he could make her. Misty held up her purse and said, "I never leave home without it. I'd rather catch a case than a funeral." He shook his head in approval. "If you ever have to use it you call me immediately. Do you understand?" He said in a very stern voice. Misty knew that her father worried about her. "Yes, Daddy. I understand completely. You told me this when you first gave it to me." Misty said in her Daddy's girl voice. "Alright, I'm just making sure." He said.

"Alright Daddy, I need a blunt, so I'm about to go. Thank you for letting me vent. I had a pretty emotional night last night, and I needed to ease my mind. You always make me feel so much better. I love you, Daddy." Misty gave her dad a big hug, and he hugged back really tight. "I love you too, Honey." He said. He walked her to the car as always. "Alright Daddy, see you later." She said. "Alright Honey, be safe. I love you." "I love you, too." She said as she drove off.

He stood there in the driveway for a minute. He worried about his Honey, but he knew better than anybody that she could not be controlled because she was exactly like him.

Chapter Seven

OPTIONS

After talking to her Daddy, Misty felt so much better. He always made her feel like she could take on the world. Driving back to the block, she was trying to figure out what she was going to do for the rest of the day. It was 1pm on a Saturday afternoon, there were a few tracks that were open. She thought to herself. She decided that for now she was just going to go smoke.

Just then her phone rang, it was Scrappe. "Shit, I forgot to text him," she said aloud. "Hello mean guy," she answered. "I'm not mean I just know how and when to put a bitch in her place. Don't you agree?" He said sarcastically. "I guess, I would definitely have to agree. And I apologize for not texting you this morning when I got in." Misty said in a submissive tone. "Apology accepted. Don't let it happen again. Do you understand?" Scrappe said sternly. "You say that as if I'm your bitch." Misty said with a hint of feistiness. "No, I say it like you agreed to do it and I expected it to happen." He said. "It's not like you gave me much of a choice." Misty said trying to defend herself. "You always have a choice. You just chose to submit instead of fight and I like that. It's a start, you're making progress." He said. Choosing to ignore what his statement insinuated, Misty said, "I just left my dad's house, I am on my way back to the house to go smoke and sort out the rest of my day." "Come over here and smoke wit me." Scrappe said. "I can do that, give me like ten minutes. Do you have Hennessy or Remy over there?" Misty asked. "I have both. See you when you get here." He hung up. As soon as the phone hung up she wished she hadn't agreed. She wasn't ready to start anything with Scrappe, just yet. She needed to make this short and brief.

"I see you lookin' like a real Garr Star today." He said as he opened the door. "That I do, cuzz that I am." Misty replied. "I never asked you last night. How was your night?" Scrappe asked. "I hit my mark, then I came in." Misty answered, trying not to elaborate. She was hoping that he didn't dig any deeper. "That's good. Did you hit the track?" He asked. Misty wanted to know why he was asking about her night. "For a minute I did. Why are you asking about my night?" She said. "I'm just wondering if all fuss is true. Cuzz niggaz act like you got platinum pussy and the money to go with it." Scrappe replied. That made Misty laugh. "Is that right? Is that what you call it? Because personally I think they act like a bunch of emotional ass niggaz that didn't know how to keep me, and now they wanna cry about it, and act like I did something wrong by leaving they ass. But that is neither here nor there. I made $750 off of the track, $1000 out of the hotel, and $200 off of a call. So does that answer your question?" Misty said. Scrappe didn't respond. He passed her the blunt and went to get two glasses and a bottle of Remy. Misty gently grabbed the bottle and glasses from him and poured their drinks. "Thank you." Scrappe said, as he held up his glass and took a sip. Misty did the same. "Do you have any lime by chance?" Misty asked. "Actually, I don't. It's time to go shopping." He said. "No problem".

"So why don't you have a woman?" Misty asked. "Who said I didn't?" Scrappe replied. "No one. It just doesn't look like a woman has anything to do with this house, except for the cleaning." She said. "Very observant, I kicked her out about two months ago and redid everything except my daughter's room." He said. "That's what's up. Look Scrappe, I'm going to be straight with you because I see where this is going and I am not ready to fuck wit you and I probably won't be anytime soon." Misty said. "That's what you think, huh? We'll see. But for now I got some business to take care of. Are we still in agreeance that you are to call me and let me know when and where you are working?" He asked. "I don't think, I know. And yes we are. I will text you." Misty said.

They were both walking to the door. Scrappe grabbed her arm and made her face him and said, "You will be mines, sooner than later." Misty took a deep breath to compose herself, then said, "I will be yours when I decide to be and not a moment sooner." Scrappe let out a cynical giggle and said, "Don't worry, you'll learn." Turning to walk out of the door Misty said, "I'm sure I will, as will you. Talk to you later."

When Misty got back to the house it was about 2:30 and she felt like she needed to eat. Just as she was about to walk into the kitchen there was a knock on the door. "Who is it?" From the other side he said, "It's Lil Giz." Misty remembered him from high school. She had a huge crush on him, but had not seen him since, and wondered if he would remember her. She opened the door. "Hey what's up? Giz ain't here, I don't know where dat nigga at or when he gon be here cuzz I just walked in. By the look on his face Misty could tell that he was digging her. "Yeah, I know. I just spoke to him. He is on his way, but he said that if the Benz is here that you were here." He said. "Oh ok, I will be gone in minute. I have business to tend to, but I'm sure that I will see you around." Misty said. "Ok, Mami. You be safe out there." He said as he took a seat on the sofa. When Misty came back out of the room she had changed out of her jeans into a skirt. Instead of the forces she had on a pair of flat green sandals and a pair of strappy, green heels in her hand. She sat her heels and purse on the coffee table and went back into the room. This time she came out with a duffle bag and a blunt.

"You wanna smoke wit me before I go?" She asked Lil Giz. "Sure, why not." He replied. Checking out the switch Lil Giz said, "What kind of business do you have to handle lookin' like that?" Misty replied sharply, "The kind that keeps me looking like this." Just as she said that Giz walked through the door. "What up Cuzz? A Cuzzo, you leaving again?" He looked at Lil Giz, then to Misty. "Yep, I got shit to do. I might be back tonight or maybe in the morning. I will keep you posted." Misty said. "Alright Cuzzo, G-safe. Call me if you need me and I love you." She gave Giz a kiss on the cheek and said, "I will, I will, and I love you, too." She waved to Lil Giz, "Alright Lil Giz, good seeing you again." "Alright Mami, you take care." He said. And Misty was gone again.

Misty decided to go to the Marina and walk around, have a bite to eat, and pass out cards. Around five o'clock she got bored so she decided to hit the track for a while. She figured that Long Beach Blvd. would be cool at this time.

As soon as she parked she seen him. He was about 5'10", medium build, medium skin tone, brown hair, a low cut, and a boyish face, that he tried to hide with a clean goatee. She acted as if she didn't notice him and walked right by his car. He passed her first test. "I see you Lil Mama," was all he said.

A little while later she thought to herself, "damn it's been almost three hours and this nigga hasn't given me his number yet. Fuck it, I been out here way too long, his lost." As she was walking to the car she seen him drive by and made it a point to make sure that he seen her looking at him. As she was getting in the car he pulled up, rolled his window down, gave her his number and pulled off. Before she could get in the car all of the way the phone was ringing and he answered.

"Damn, you're fast. Are you in that much of a hurry to choose?" He said. Misty laughed "Well shit, I was waiting for three hours for you to give me your number, which was two hours longer than I planned on being on this cheap ass track." "It's ok Ma, it builds work ethic. What's ya name? Mines is C.J." He said. "Nice to meet you C.J., my name is Misty. Could we possibly meet up and have a drink?" She said. "That depends Misty, are you choosing or playing?" He said. "Sweetie, I don't play and I could be choosing but since I don't choose strangers we gon have to do some conversing first." Misty said. "I hear you sweetie, let me take care of some things and I will call you in about an hour." C.J. said. "Alright, but just to be curious, what is your fee?" Misty asked. "Come wit five and we can talk." C.J. said. Misty paused for a second because she wasn't expecting such a low number, then said, "oh, ok. Well, I will be in Hollywood. I have a room at the Standard on Sunset for the night." Misty said. "That's a bet. See you in a little while Ma." He said.

Ok, I have $700 on me, I am going to stop at the house, grab another outfit and some weed, then hit Sunset for a couple of hours, and be at the Standard by 12. Or should I get the room first, then hit the track? Yeah, that's what I will do. So, she got the room and was down on Sunset by 10. C.J. called her at 10:30, but she was busy so she sent him a text back. "Getting some dough, I will be ready for you shortly." He texted back, "Bet". Then she remembered Scrappe. She simply texted, "on Sunset" and he replied with a simple "7x" .

She noticed that she had two missed calls from an unfamiliar number, so she called it back. "Misty, I am so glad that you returned my call. This is Shawn, how soon can you be here? I have a friend that is dieing to meet you." He said. "Hey Shawn, it is 10:45 right now. I can be there by 11:15. Are we meeting at the bar or in your room?" Misty asked. "My room, we are waiting." He hung up.

She made it back to the Standard with 15 minutes to spare. She went to the bar and handed something to the bartender, then made a call to C.J. "May I ask what you drink?" she said. "Perfect, I will be ready at 1am, room 327. Get the key from the bartender, just tell him that Misty is waiting." And she hung up.

Finally, I'm going to get some pimp dick tonight, I can't wait. Pimps always got swipe, and they are the only niggaz that fuck me right!!!!!!!

Chapter Eight

PIMP DICK MAKES A REAL HOE

WEAK

Misty ran to valet because she had to put the rest of her money in the car. Then, she ran back up to the room to get ready for C.J.

She was just getting out of the shower when she heard the door open. "I'll be out in a minute. Help yourself to a drink." She yelled from the bathroom. He looked around and seen the Remy bottle sitting on the nightstand, next to two glasses, a wave of hundreds sitting under it, and two blunts sitting next to it. "I like this bitch." He said to himself. He poured two drinks and sat at the desk next to the bed.

Misty walked out of the bathroom wearing red boyshorts, a white and red tank top, hair down and wet, lips glossed, and smelling like cotton blossom.

C.J. just stared for a minute. "Where the fuck did you come from?" He asked in a puzzled but excited voice. "I suppose I came from my mother and father." Misty said in a sweet voice, as she sat indian style on the bed facing him. "Is that right bitch? So how old are you? Where are you from? Who have you fucked with? Tell me about yourself. Light one of those blunts, sip your drink, and talk to me." He said.

They talked for about an hour, exchanging life stories, and then the question came. "So tell me do you wanna fuck wit me or do you just wanna fuck me. I'm cool with either or. I just don't wanna leave here in the morning thinking that I have another woman on my team and I really don't." He asked. "Since you put it like that I will be honest with you. My intentions tonight were to come here get fucked real good and then be gone. But I would actually like to get to know you further and possibly fuck with you." Misty said as she reached for the other blunt. He grabbed her hand and locked it above her head. Looking into her eyes he said, "I love your honesty. And there is no possibly. When I put that money in my pocket and stick my dick in every hole on your body you will belong to me." He let that settle into her thoughts for a few moments and then whispered into her ear, "Do I make myself clear?" She whispered, "Yes." "Yes, what?" He said sternly. "Yes, C.J." she said. He grabbed her by the throat and looked into her eyes. She closed her eyes. "Open your fuckin eyes and look at me, bitch. Now I said, yes what. And don't play with me." "Yes, Daddy." She said. "Do you want to pay me now and every day from now on?" he said. "Yes, Daddy." She said. "Do you want to feel my dick inside of you?" He asked. "Yes, Daddy" she said. "Then prove it bitch." He let her go.

Misty reached over to the nightstand a grabbed the money and handed it to him. He counted it. Then set it back on the nightstand. He paused for a few seconds, then gave Misty a sharp slap in the face. "You got one more chance, and bitch please do not play with me." He said. Misty said "Yes, Daddy." Then opened the nightstand drawer, grabbed the phone book and took hundred dollar bills out of ten random pages, and handed them to him. "I'm......." He slapped her again and cut off her apology. "That's better, now prove the rest." Misty undid his pants and when his dick finally got free from his boxers, she was very pleased. She gave him the best head that she could give him until he grabbed her by her hair and flipped her over on her back and started kissing her passionately. As he was kissing her he said, "Are you my bitch?" "Yes, Daddy I'm your bitch." She replied. "Are you my hoe?" he asked. "Yes, Daddy I'm your hoe." She replied. He then went down and his tongue and her clit played a game together that sent her up the wall. When she couldn't take it anymore she grabbed his head and pulled him up and said, "I'm your bitch Daddy. Please fuck me now? I need to feel you inside of me." "Are you sure that you are ready for me bitch?" he asked. "Yes, Daddy I am ready Daddy. Please fuck me." And he plunged inside of her like the secret to life was between her legs and he had to dig it out. For the next three hours he fucked her like she had never been fucked before in her life.

It was close to 6am and Misty didn't know rather she wanted to go get down or go home. C.J. really threw her for a loop. She kind of wanted to give him a chance. Fuck it, why not. She thought. She asked him if he could pick her up from Gardena around 3pm, and she would text him the address. He agreed and she packed up her stuff in the room and they left the hotel.

When she got back to the house she was kind of nervous. She didn't know how to tell Giz that she chose up by accident. He was going to be pissed, but she knew that he would be ok.

It was only 7:30am when she got back to the house. Giz was still asleep, so Misty climbed in the bed with him and dozed off. A short while later she felt him move and her eyes popped open. "I need to talk to you Cuzz." She said. "Shoot, I'm listening." He replied. "I think that I accidently chose up last night." She said. There was silence. Misty got up and went and put her coffee in the microwave. When she walked back in the room she had her coffee in one hand and a cigarette in the other hand. "So tell me how you accidently choose, 'cause that sounds hella stupid to me. But maybe I just don't understand." Giz said. She told him the entire story. "Are you addicted to paying pimps or something? 'Cause I know a bunch of niggaz that will fuck you good for free, if that's all you want." Giz said. "Honestly Cuzz, it turns me on and I don't know why. It's like some kind of disease or something. I think I need to go to Paying Pimps Anonymous." Misty said. "So you gave that nigga all of the money that you had on you?" Giz asked. Misty looked at him crazy. "Hell naw, I put two racks in the car before he got there. It started off as me just wanting to fuck a pimp, but I actually liked him, so I chose up. But, now I am second guessing my decision. Don't trip, I'll figure it out. I'm still gon be here though, but he gon pick me up at three. That way you can meet him and give me your opinion of him." Misty explained. Giz looked really confused and said, "Aiight Cuzzo, you know I'm ready to go at anytime. That's all I gotta say." Misty already knew that so all she said was, "Fasho, Cuzz."

That conversation was easier than Misty thought it was going to be. Now she just had to figure out how to get C.J. to let her stay living with Giz and still fuck with him. Three o'clock came quick. Misty's phone rang. She answered and said, "Come inside, I'm not ready yet." Not giving C.J. a chance to object she hung up. "Cuzz, he's here. He is about to come in. I will be out of the room in a few minutes, I need to finish getting ready." She said to Giz."

"What up cuzz, Giz." He introduced himself as soon as he opened the door. "C.J. my nigga." He said. "Aiight, Misty will be out in a few minutes, I guess." Giz said. Getting straight to the point, Giz continued to speak. "Look homie, I don't really know much about this pimp and hoe shit. And honestly I don't give a fuck about it, but Misty is my fam so just know that I will do damage over her without question. So look out for her and keep her safe." C.J. was kind of caught off guard by that. "She gon be good fam. You don't have to worry, I don't even plan on having her out there like that. As a matter of fact I will bring her back in the morning so that she can let you know what's up." C.J. said. Giz shook his hand and said, "Good lookin', I appreciate that." "No problem" C.J. said.

About an hour later Misty and C.J. pulled up to an auto shop. "What's wrong with your car?" Misty asked. "Nothing Ma, I work here. And this place is full of Mexicans wit money. They will mostly want quickies. Don't do shit for less than $100. I will be done around 8. Let's see if you can out trap me." He shot her a wink and a smile. "So, when I win, what do I get?" Misty asked

very confidently. "What makes you think that you are

going to win?" C.J. said. "You'll see." Misty said with a

smirk on her face.

As soon as they walked in Misty seen what kind

of shop it was. It was a chop shop and from the looks of

it, they had plenty of business. C.J. did the radio

installations and some of the foot work.

At 8:15 C.J. said, "Are you ready to go?" "I sure

am." Misty said with a smirk on her face. They got in the

car and Misty said, "I need a shower. But anyways what

did you get?" "No, no, no you first." C.J. said. "That's not

fair, but whatever. Here is the $600 I would have got at

your rate, and here is the other $600 that I got at my

rate. Now, what did you get?" Misty crossed her legs

and gave him a look like, now what. "Aiight, Lil Mama, I

see you. You did that. You got me this time, but next

time I'm gon win." C.J. said as he backed the car out.

"So how much did you get?" Misty asked. "Not as much

as you. I ain't never had a bitch get more than $800 out

of there." He said. "Well, if a bitch settles for less then

that is what she gets, but I don't fuck for less than $200

and I knew they had it so that is what they gave me.

Anyways, what do I win?" Misty said. "You win a night

with Daddy, that's what." He said then turned the music

up.

A short while later they pulled up to an extended

stay hotel. Misty didn't say anything but she was damn

sure thinking it. "If this nigga thinks that he is about to

have me staying here then he has me entirely fucked

up" she thought to herself. Sensing that Misty was not feeling this C.J. said, "I just lost my house about a month ago. I'm not used to livin' like this, but it's temporary. Just bare wit me." Feeling a little bad Misty said, "Was my disgust that obvious?" "Yes, it was very obvious, but I like that. It let's me know that you gon get it to make our situation better. But listen, I got three bitches up here that you about to meet and all of them got issues. Just let me handle it." He said.

Misty took a deep breath and said, "Ok, but I don't like bitches and they don't like me either, and I don't have time or tolerance for games. So maybe you should just drop me off at the house and we can link back up after the night is over." C.J. stopped walking and pulled her close to him and said, "You have paid me more in 24 hours than all three of these bitches have paid me in three days, put together. If they got a problem wit you then they can all shake. Now come on."

One of Misty's pet peeves was when a pimp put money over loyalty. She usually made it a point to make an example out of niggaz like that by letting him push his bitches aside and when they leave she would leave him feeling stupid. But she kind of liked him and did not want to do him like that.

When they walked in she got the normal fake greetings that bitches gave. She played along, for the sake of keeping the peace, but she was highly irritated. One bitch looked mixed with a nice complexion, and good hair, but no body. Her name was Star. She was his "bottom." Another bitch looked fresh out of the projects and was trying to looked mixed to compete with the other bitch, her name was Mia. Then there was another bitch that just looked out of place. Misty could not understand why she was even there. She was fat, unshapely, and dark skinned, her name was Shay. They were all dressed and ready to go get down. That was cool with Misty because she needed to make some money so that she could stuff some and bring it home.

C.J. broke up the introductions, "I am glad to see you ladies are getting along, but y'all need to go get some money and Misty, didn't you say that you needed a shower?" Misty grabbed her bag and said, "Yes, Daddy. I do." as she walked towards the bathroom. She could tell that the bitches were pissed off. Before she closed the door she heard Star say, "We can wait for her to get ready."

When she got out of the shower C.J. was laying in the bed. She looked at him and said, "So where are we going tonight? Hollywood should be good right now." C.J. smiled and said, "You worked enough today. Come lay down wit Daddy." Misty took a deep breath. "Here you go with the deep breath. What is the problem?" He asked "Okay, look. I know how the game goes. And I know that other bitches shouldn't bother me but they do. Now some things I will get past and accept. But I am not going to sit on, lay on, or touch another woman's bed, let alone three. So, can we leave?" Misty explained. C.J. did not budge not one inch. "Look, I need to get some sleep. So chill out and lay down. I will get you your own room in the morning."

He said. C.J. had no idea what type of bitch he was

dealing with, but he was about to find out. Misty simply

said, "Ok, get some rest, but I'm not getting in that

bed."

Five minutes later he was sleep. Ten minutes

later Misty was in the parking lot talking to a trick.

Twenty minutes later Misty was at the house getting

dressed for Hollywood.

Chapter Nine

POW! YOU CAN'T ALWAYS RUN

"What's up Cuzzo? B.J. said he wasn't bringing you back until the morning. What happened?" Giz asked "His name is C.J., and he clearly had me mistaken. He really thought that I was going to lay with him at a room with one bed that he shared with three other bitches. Them other bitches can go for that, but not I." Misty said with that feisty attitude. "So what? You had him drop you off?" Giz asked. "Hell naw. He said he needed a nap, so I let him sleep and I got the fuck on. I don't got time to be arguing wit no nigga over what I'm not gon do. That's why I be leaving these niggaz. A bitch can't win no argument wit a pimp. And bottom line is that I do what I want, when I want, and where I want. And I make the money to do so, so when these niggaz don't give me my way, I get on my way. These niggaz betta check my bloodline and figure out who the fuck they dealin' wit." Misty said as she lit a blunt. "GarrGarr, and that's what it do Cuzzo." Giz said.

After they smoked the blunt Misty said, "Aiight Cuzz, I'm about to go for the night. I got money to collect and I know it's waiting for me to come get it." "A Cuzzo, let me ask you a question." Giz said. "I'm listening" Misty replied. "You don't be scared that one of these niggaz is gon catch up with you and do something?" He asked. "Cuzz, you know me better than anybody. Have you ever known me to be scared of anything? And have you ever seen me not hold my own? I'm ready for whatever comes my way in these streets, and I stay heated at all times. So, if one of these niggaz really want it then trust me I will not hesitate to give it to 'em. And the reality is that these niggaz want to get me back not hurt me. So when I run across them I give them just enough to give them hope that I will come back, then I'm gone again. It's all a game and I play it well. Don't worry, I got this. And if all else fails, I know I got goons ready to go at any given moment." Misty gave him a kiss on the cheek, grabbed her purse, keys and hygiene bag. All Giz could say was, "Aiight Cuzzo, G-safe, I love you." Misty said, "I love you too Cuzz." And she was out the door.

It was almost 11. Misty decided to play the track all night. She played her favorite corner at the top of Sunset, right across the street from 7-11. By 3am Misty had $900, which wasn't great for her, but it was cool. She figured another two hours and she would head to the house.

She went to the car to drop off the money and freshen up a bit. She checked her phone and she had twelve missed calls. Nine of them were from C.J., and three of them were from Scrappe. She decided to call C.J. back. "So you just said fuck me right." He said as soon as he answered his phone. "It's not like that. I just don't indulge in low budget shit.. But can we discuss this over lunch tomorrow because I'm busy, I just wanted to return your call." Misty said. Then she realized that he had already hung up. Oh well, she thought and then put her phone back in her purse.

As she was about to get out, the passenger door flew open, and before she could say anything a fist flew into her right temple and the left side of her head hit the window. Then there was a hand around her throat. "Bitch, you thought I was playing wit you. You can't leave me bitch."

When her eyes came into focus, she seen Shorty in front of her face. Now she was pissed because not only was she going to have to stop her night because of this knot that she felt growing on her head, but she was also going to have to give him the money that she just made, so that he would leave her alone. She got caught slipping so she had to pay. She knew and understood that. But all she could think was that he didn't have to hit her.

"Look Shorty, I only got $900 on me, you can have it. Can you just leave me alone, now?" Misty said with an attitude. He socked her in the jaw and said, "Bitch, this ain't about the money. I told you that you was mines forever, and I meant that." Misty could see the tears in his eyes.

For the first time Misty found herself in a situation that money or charm could not get her out of. And she knew from stories that Unique told that Shorty thought he could beat a bitch into submission. Up until now, the most a nigga, besides her turn out folks, has ever done to Misty was slap and choke her. And that turned her on so it really didn't do shit.

"This nigga has lost his rabbit ass mind." Misty thought to herself. The side of her face hurt, but she could tell that her jaw wasn't broke. She figured that she would try one more time to handle the situation like a typical hoe would handle it. But she defied herself as the words came out of her mouth. "Nigga you got me fucked up. You got one mo………."

It all seemed to happen in slow motion. Before she could finish her sentence, the back of his hand was in her mouth, and her pistol was pointed at his head. "Oh, so you a bad bitch now. Bitch, you gon shoot me?" He said, in a slightly lower tone than he was using before.

Misty knew that once she pulled out, the rest was a wrap. She was taught that if you pull it out, then you use it. "Nigga, I was born a bad bitch." "POW!!!"

Misty reached over him, opened the passenger side door, pushed him out and smashed off.

The closest freeway was too far for her to drive with his brains and blood all over the window. So she pulled down the first dark street she seen and cleaned the window the best that she could with feminine wipes.

She grabbed her phone, "Daddy, are you at home?" she asked. "Yeah, Honey. What's wrong?" he said. "I'll tell you when I get there." She hung up.

Surprisingly, she wasn't as shook up as she thought she should be. And that scared her more than anything. When she hit the freeway, she lit a cigarette, rolled the windows down, and turned on Plies full blast.

When she pulled up to her dad's, she grabbed her duffle bag out of the trunk, and went in the house. Germ was sitting on the couch smoking a cigarette, with a drink in his hand. She handed him the gun and the keys and said, "The car needs to be cleaned and I need a shower and a blunt." He kissed her on the forehead and said, "Ok." Then he went outside and she went straight to the bathroom.

Looking in the mirror, she could see that the side of her face was swollen, she had a huge knot on the left side of her forehead, and the inside of her mouth was cut up. At that moment she wished that the nigga was still alive so that she could pistol whip him and then shoot him.

When she got out of the shower her dad was sitting on the couch. He handed her a blunt and said, "Courtesy of P.B.. He said that he will be back in an hour or two with the car as good as new. Now would you like to tell me what happened?" He said.

Misty lit the blunt and told her dad the whole story. He looked at her and said, "It sounds to me like he got off easy cuzz I would have tortured the muthafucka." He got up and walked to the kitchen and when he came back he handed Misty a bag of peas wrapped in a paper towel. "Here put that on your face. Honey, I wish that you would just find a nice guy and settle down with him. I don't like this shit at all. My baby should not be out here killin niggaz. It's just not right." He said in a very melancholy voice. "Daddy, like it or not I'm your daughter and I'm just like you. And I don't want a nice guy I want a pimp that's a gangsta. And the next nigga that put his hands on me gon get the same thing that nigga got. Speaking of, I need another pistol." Misty said with an attitude. Knowing that every word that she said was true and feeling half way responsible, if not completely responsible for the way his daughter was he simply said, "I know Honey, I know. When P.B. brings the car back he will have another pistol for you too." Misty got up and sat in her dad's lap like a big baby, and he cradled her like one. "Daddy, do you know what scares me more than anything?" She asked "What is that Honey?" He said "I don't feel anything, nothing at all. If it wasn't for my face and the mess in the car I would have parked somewhere else and kept working." She said. He hugged her tighter and

said, "That scares me too Honey."

Chapter Ten

WHEN LIFE TAKES A TOLL

P.B. didn't get back until close to 11. "What's up

killa?" He said to Misty as he walked through the door.

"You can call me Baby, like you always do. What took

you so long?" Misty shot back. "Damn, can a nigga get a thank you or something?" He said. "I'm sorry. Thank you. I love you so much." Misty said apologetically. "He winked at her and said, "You know Daddy got cha back. Come take a ride wit me and you can tell me what happened."

P.B. was about 6', 270 lbs., and about the same complexion as Misty. He was Germ's little homie and a cold hustler. Him and Misty always had a thing for one another, but out of respect for her father they never got together. That didn't stop them from flirting, though.

"So, where we going?" Misty asked as she jumped in his Hummer. "I just have a few runs to make, then we gotta pick up your pistol at 2." He said. "Damn, I gotta kill a nigga for you to spend a few hours wit me. I might have to do that more often." Misty said, with a smirk on her face. "Naw, don't do that. I just be busy Baby. You know that. Don't take it personal. So tell me what happened."

She told him the entire story. They were stopped at a light and he reached over and gently grabbed her face and turned it so he could see. "He is definitely lucky that he only had you to deal with. Why you be playin wit niggaz like that? This shit was bound to happen sooner or later." He said. "Maybe if you would stop playin and make me yo bitch shit like this wouldn't happen. Don't get me started P.B.." She said. "Alright, alright, alright. Chill out young grasshopper. What you feel like eating? We got a couple of hours to spare." P.B. said. "I don't care, somewhere with a bar because I don't really have an appetite, but I can use a drink, or two, or three."

Misty said.

"That's cool. I'll pay cuzz I found this $900 this morning that I am dieing to spend." He said. "Yeah, ok nigga. You better gimme my money. As a matter of fact, you can keep that. I should probably give you more." Misty said. He put the money in her lap and said, "When you pay me it will be because you are my bitch and that is what you are supposed to do. What I did this morning was because, above all, I am your friend and that is what I was supposed to do. Now come on and let's go have a drink."

He put the truck in park and they hopped out. They went in and shot a few games of pool and had a few drinks. P.B.'s phone rang and he said, "Let's go."

Without question Misty gulped the rest of her drink and they were out of there.

"We going to pick up my pistol?" Misty asked. "Yep, then I'm dropping you off because I got shit to do." He said. Misty smiled and said, "I love you, and you will never understand how much." "I love you, too Baby." Was all he said. They chit chatted about random shit on the way. But they were both thinking the same thing. And that was that they would be great together, and too bad that it would never be. But above all they both valued their friendship extremely.

After they got the pistol, he dropped her back off at Germ's. Misty went in told her dad thank you and that she'll see him later. And she was out of there.

She checked her phone and she had a missed call from Giz. She called him right back. "What's up Cuzz?" She said when she heard his voice on the other end. "A Cuzzo, where you at? This nigga Scrappe is over here and he is furious. He keep saying something about a pimp being shot and you not answering your phone. I don't know what the fuck is going on, but you need to call him or something." Giz said. "I'm on my way. I'm leaving the hood right now, so give me about ten minutes. Tell dat nigga to chill out." Misty said, then hung up.

Damn, I wonder if that nigga put it together. And if he put it together, then who else would. Oh well, fuck it. Can't nobody prove it. She thought to herself.

She stopped at the store and got a bottle of

Remy and a pack of swishers. She was going to be in the house for the next couple of days waiting for her face to go down, and she planned on being fucked up the entire time.

When she walked through the door Scrappe gave her a look that could have killed. "Damn, what the fuck did I do to you." Misty snapped at Scrappe. "You don't answer yo mutha fuckin phone. That's what! Why have the mutha fucka if you not gon answer it. I seen you down last night then all of the commotion started and I didn't see you anymore. And when you wouldn't answer your phone I got worried." Scrappe said in a very angry tone. "Well, I am fine. I keep my phone on silent and check it when I get ready to and I call back who I feel like, when I feel like. It's my phone, I pay the bill so that is my right. Now, do you have any weed cuzz I need to smoke."Misty snapped again. It took everything inside of Scrappe not to knock fire from Misty. He kept his cool because he knew how Giz felt about her. "The weed is at the house. Come on, let's go get it. You drive."

Scrappe had every intention on slapping her as soon as they got in the car. Then he seen the side of her face. Then he smelled the fumes inside of the car. He then started paying attention to other minor details. He chose not to say a word.

"Go ahead, I know you wanna let me have it for the way that I spoke to you in there, and for not checking in with you last night. Just get it over with now, please." Misty said sarcastically. "Don't worry about it.

It's ok." Scrappe said.

When they walked in the house Scrappe said, "Toss me those keys. I think I left something in the car." Misty tossed him the keys and sat down. He went outside and took a closer look at the passenger side and confirmed his suspicions. He opened the gate and the garage and pulled it inside. Then, he went back into the house. When he walked in he looked at Misty and shook his head, then said, "You a cold piece of work." Misty looked back at him and said, "Tell me something I don't know. And are you almost ready to go because I am ready to get fucked up." "Alright give me five minutes and we outta here. But you really should just stay wit me for a few days."Scrappe said. "I bet that would be right up your alley, but no thank you. I think I need to be at home." Misty said.

Scrappe didn't argue with her. He simply went and got some weed and said, "Let's go." He threw her the keys to his car and said, "It needs to be cleaned better and it needs to be off of the scene for a while, and so do you." Misty said nothing, she just caught the keys and went to the car.

She started the car and then laid her head on the steering wheel. "He gave me no other option." Misty said in a tone that gave the impression that she was beginning to feel remorseful. Scrappe got out of the car, walked around to her side, opened the door, stood her up and held her. They stood there like that for about seven minutes while Misty cried on his shoulder.

Misty couldn't understand why she all of a sudden felt the urge to cry, and to him of all people. But she had to admit to herself that it felt good to be in his arms. In an attempt to fight what she was feeling for Scrappe she pulled away and said, "I want to go home. I wanna be with Giz right now." They both got back in the car. "Giz can't handle this." Scrappe said. "I know, I just want to be near him. Him and my dad make me feel safe and secure, like nothing can harm me. They ease the world for me. I just want to be around him." Misty said in a soft voice that let Scrappe know that she wasn't as tough as she thought she was. "Sounds like you don't wanna be a big girl right now." He said in a teasing way. He didn't want to see her like this and he knew that would help her snap back.

"Until I find a man that gives me the same sense of security and worth that they give me, I will continue to be a big girl. Don't let this little moment fool you because as quick as it came, it is now gone. Do you have Plies in here?" Misty said as she searched through the different artist on the screen.

Scrappe just left well enough alone. He pushed her hand out of the way and found Plies for her. He knew that she needed guidance, but now was not the time to give it to her. Right now she needed love and support.

When they got back to the house Misty changed into some oversized sweats and a green Pro club. She put her hair in two braids. Then she curled up on the couch and waited for Scrappe to finish rolling a blunt.

"Is somebody gon fuckin tell me what the fuck is going on?" Giz said. Misty had always been able to tell Giz anything, but she wasn't sure if she wanted to tell him what was going on. She couldn't lie to him though.

"That nigga Shorty caught me slippin last night, bringing some money to the car. He thought he was about to just beat up on me. I gave him a warning and he hit me again, so I put a bullet in his head in the passenger seat of your car. My Dad had the homie take it and get it cleaned. And get rid of the pistol and get me another one. Scrappe said it needed to be cleaned better, so it's in his garage and I'm driving his car. Now, can somebody light the blunt?" Misty said.

"What the fuck, are you serious? That nigga hit you? Let me see your face. Are you sure that nigga is dead, cuzz on Dragnet Gang I'll kill dat mutha fucka.

Cuzz, you ain't going out by yourself no mo. I don't give

a fuck." Giz is hyped up now. Scrappe shook his head.

Misty shrugged her shoulders and hit the blunt.

Over the next few months Misty and Scrappe

became very close. She fell in love with the way that he

took control. With him she didn't feel like she had to do

everything herself. She even began to let her guard

down and do things his way, and she actually liked it.

Giz wasn't sure how to take in Misty and Scrappe

being together. Something just didn't set right with him,

but he figured that they were grown, and as long as he

didn't harm her that it was cool.

"Daddy, I wanna go to Vegas for a few days."

Misty said to Scrappe. "We can do that, you'll probably trap nice out there." He replied. "Yeah, but I wanna go for play, not work." Misty whined. "It's not playtime yet, but you can definitely go out there to get some dough." He said. Misty took a deep breath, grabbed her purse, and keys, and said, "I'm going to see what Giz is doing." As she was walking to the door Scrappe grabbed her hand and said, "We not gon start that spoiled shit. Do you understand?" Misty took another deep breath and said, "Yes Daddy, I understand. Now, can I go?" He let her go and she walked out the door.

The same things that Misty and Scrappe loved about each other were the same things that were driving them apart. Misty loved that she could depend on him to control a situation, but was getting annoyed that he felt he had to control every one. And Scrappe loved that Misty was so strong minded but thought that she should tone it down when it came to him.

"A Cuzz, I gotta put some distance between me and Scrappe before shit goes real bad real fast because this submissive shit is getting old and irritating." Misty said to Giz. "I don't know what to tell you Cuzzo. Shit, just do what makes you happy." Giz said. "I'm thinking about to go to Vegas." She said. "When you plan on going? We got a few homies out there if you wanna hit 'em up when you get there." Giz said. "I might push tonight. I'm trying to see what Scrappe say, but you know me." Misty said. "Damn, why so soon?" He asked. "Because I'm grown and when I woke up this morning that's where I felt like I wanted to be." Misty said with a bit of an attitude. "A Cuzzo, you already know that whatever you do, I got cha back." Giz said. "And that's why I love you." She said as she kissed him on the cheek. Then she left.

She checked her phone and seen a missed call from Unique. She wondered what that was about, so she called back. "A, what's up? You called?" She said when she heard Unique answer. "Misty, oh my God. I don't know what to do without Shorty. I have had five different Pimps in the last six months and I am going crazy." Unique said. "Have you ever been to Vegas?" Misty asked. "No, why is that where you are?" Unique replied. "No, but that is where I'm going. Get your shit together. Text me your address, and I will call you when I am on my way." Misty said, and then hung up.

She just had to figure out how to get away from Scrappe without incident. When she got to the house, he was gone, so that was easy enough. She didn't have much there so it didn't take long to grab her stuff and get out the door. When she got back to Giz spot she packed some more things and grabbed five racks out of her stash, that had grown to a little over fifty racks. She kissed Giz and said, "Aiight Cuzz, I'm leaving Scrappe's car here and taking yours. I will bring it back as soon as I buy me one. I'm about to go though." "Damn, you going to Vegas already, it ain't even been thirty minutes." Giz said. "You know me Cuzz, my mind was already made up. And I ain't got the patients to argue wit Scrappe, so I have to hurry up and leave while he is busy." Misty said. "So you not fuckin wit Cuzz no mo or what?" Giz asked.

"I'm fuckin wit myself. All that nigga want is for me to do what he say when he say it and what I want doesn't matter. That shit was cool for a minute because my mind was fucked up and else where, but now I am over it. I am back to being myself and I gotta go do me." Misty said. "Alright Cuzzo. You going by yourself?" Giz asked. "The Unique bitch called me crying earlier. She is a fucking idiot, can't do shit on her own. I feel kind of responsible considering why she is alone. So I'm gon take her with me. But alright, let me go. I'll call you when I get there." Misty said. "G careful Cuzzo. I'm gon hit Lil Giz up and let him know you coming out there. As a matter of fact put his number in your phone." Giz said. "Just text it to me Cuzz, I gotta go before Scrappe realize I'm gone. I love you. I'll call you later." Misty said as she was driving off.

Chapter Eleven

UNIQUE & VEGAS, BITCH
YOU'RE MINE; THE LIGHTS & CARPET

"I'll be there in ten minutes, be outside." Misty

said, then hung up. When Unique got in the car she

looked a hot mess. She had on a synthetic wig that

looked a year old. Her nails and toes were not done. And her clothes looked cheap as hell.

Unique was not an ugly girl, but she was no Misty. She was 5'5", about 120 lbs., medium skin tone, B-cups, with a small frame. When she was dressed and done up she could definitely hold her own.

"Bitch, where the fuck have you been? You look horrible." Misty said when Unique got in the car. "I told you that I have been going through it since Shorty got shot." Unique said. "It looks like you been going through more than it. But I guess. How much money you got?" Misty said with disgust in her voice. "I don't have any. I didn't have time to get down and put any aside." She said.

Misty almost smashed on the brakes. "You mean to tell me that you planned on going to Vegas with no money, with me. What did you plan on doing when we got there?" Misty said and she was obviously pissed off. "I don't know. I just didn't know who else to call." She said, almost in tears. "Look Unique, these streets ain't no place for a weak ass bitch, so knock off all of the whining and crying. You are a grown ass woman with a pussy, and you know how to sell it. The way you look is a fucking disgrace, and it ain't nobody's fault but your own. I don't give a fuck what nigga you are with, your upkeep is your responsibility. I'm gon tell you right now I am not about to pay your way. You have three choices. Either we stop in Pamona so you can get some money and pay your way, you can get out of the car right now, or you can be my hoe and give me everything from this point on. Make your decision now because I need to know what freeway to get on." Misty said in a very authoritative voice. "I don't know." Unique mumbled. "Wow, do you know anything? I'll tell you what. We gon go with the last option. For now on you are my hoe. Now we still about to stop in Pamona and you gon make a G before we head to Vegas." Misty did not wait for a response. She turned up the music and pushed it.

They made it to Pamona around 1, it was now 5 and Unique had only made $360. It was Friday and Misty was getting pissed. "Bitch, just come on cuzz at this rate we gon be here until tomorrow." Misty said. "It was slow Misty." Unique said. "Don't trip cuzz when we get there you are going straight to the track as soon as we get off the freeway. And you will be down all night while I'm on the strip." Misty exclaimed. "Why can't I work the strip with you?" Unique asked. "You will start working the strip as soon as you make at least a G off of the track. As of right now you are not strip material and I am not spending my money, from my pussy, on you. So if you wanna work the strip then get some real money and you can." Misty said.

It was 8:30 when they got to Vegas and Misty needed a blunt and a nap. She checked her phone and Scrappe had been calling non-stop all day. She decided to deal with him after she put Unique down.

"Alright Unique, this is Tropicana. You work it

like you work any other track. Stay in between the freeway and two major streets down, which is Jones. Every 250 you get call me. When I go in this gas station you get out of the car and go to work." Misty instructed. "Ok, Misty I will call you when I got 250." Unique said eagerly.

Misty decided to get a room at Ceasars Palace for the weekend. When she got up to the room she ran a nice hot bath and rolled a blunt.

Finally she answered her phone, "Yes, Scrappe." She said. "Bitch, where the fuck are you at?" He screamed through the phone. "I am soaking in the tub, smoking a blunt." She said calmly. "You know what the fuck I mean Misty. Don't play wit me. I am not in the mood." Scrappe said forcing himself not to yell. "Who said I was playing? I told you that I wanted to go to Vegas, so that is what I did." Misty said. "Are you fucking serious? Bitch, check this out. You better drop some money in the account real soon. And it better be Vegas numbers." Scrappe said sternly. "I came out here to relax, and that is what I intend on doing. I will work when I get good and ready to work and not a moment sooner. And if I decide that I still want to pay you then we can talk numbers." Misty said nonchalantly. "And what money are you relaxing wit, cuzz I didn't give you any?" He asked. "And for some odd reason you thought that I was broke. Nigga, get real. Bye." She hung up.

Scrappe didn't even bother calling back because he knew that she would not answer. Misty had a way of pissing him off like no other bitch had ever done. If she wasn't Giz little cousin he would have been done something to her. But he was beginning to get to the point that he didn't care who she was related to.

She called Giz to let him know that she made it then she closed her eyes to relax. When she woke up and got out of the tub it was 11 o' clock. She decided to call and check on Unique. "Whats up Ma? What it look like out there?" Misty said. "It's cool. I tried to call you. I got $400 right now." Unique said excitedly. "That's good. Keep working, I will be out there in like an hour or so." Misty replied. "Ok, but can I get something to eat, because I am starving?" Unique asked. "Go grab a candy bar to hold you over. I will take you to get something to eat when I get there." Misty said then hung up.

Misty knew that she was being hard on Unique,

but she didn't feel bad because it was no harder than she would be on herself. If she was in Unique's situation she would be on the track too, no food, no sleep, nothing but dough. She felt like when you are down you got to stay down in order to come up.

Misty got to Unique a little after 1 a.m. and she had $650 by then. "Do you want to get something to eat and get back down or do you want to go to the room and call it a night?" Misty asked as soon as Unique got in the car. "I am kind of tired so I will just go back to the room and call it a night." Unique said.

When Misty dropped her off she gave her the room key and said, "Do not touch anything on my bed. There is a half a blunt on the desk. I'll be back later."

"Okay, where are you going?" Unique asked. "I'm going

to work" Misty said. "Okay, be careful." Unique said.

Misty was irritated because she could not stand when bitches took the easy way out. But she had a plan for Unique, she was going to break her out of that shit.

Misty had never actually worked the strip before. The last time she came to Vegas she was 20 and her folks at the time made her work the track. He said that he did not want to burn her out before she got a good run. She figured it would be just like working the hotel bars back at home. She had heard a lot of good things about the MGM so that was her first stop. She tipped the valet a twenty and went in. The first bar that she seen she ordered her usual, a double shot of Remy with a twist of lime, on ice. She tipped the bartender twenty and decided to walk with her drink.

The next bar that she came to she decided to sit and watch the traffic through the casino for a bit. After about thirty minutes or so she saw him, a middle aged black guy wearing simple jeans, a polo shirt, and some Nikes. What caught her eye was the platinum Cartier watch that he was wearing. He was walking in a manner that gave off the impression that he thought he wasn't drunk.

Misty grabbed her drink and acted like he was who she had been waiting on. "There you go." She announced as she slipped her arm under his. "Do I know you?" He asked. "Yes, you do. I am the woman that you have been dreaming about your entire life." Misty said and shot him a smile. "You are definitely a dream come true. Would you care for another drink?" He replied

"Yes, that would be nice. Are we having it at the bar or in your room?" Misty asked. "My room would be great. It's at Bally's. I was just about to hop in a taxi." He said. "How about I drive?" Misty asked. "That's even better. By the way, I'm Damien. And you are?" He said. "My name is Misty, it's a pleasure to meet you." Misty said.

As they got into the car Damien asked, "Is this for fun or do you have other motives?" "It's always for fun Baby. And I promise that you will have a lot of it. How long are you in town?" Misty said. "I leave tomorrow." Damien replied. "That's too bad, sorry I didn't catch you sooner." Misty said.

They sat at the bar inside of Bally's and ordered about four rounds of drinks. Misty poured two out in the bathroom and spilled one, but he drank all of his.

"Oh my Gosh, I am so fucking drunk. Let's go up to your room. And can you grab me some cash for a taxi. I do not want to drive when I leave here. I am way too blasted." Misty said in a slurred voice. "Sure Baby, I wouldn't want you to get into an accident or anything like that when you leave.

When they stopped at the ATM Misty was hanging all over him, and kissing on his neck. She was acting like she really wanted him. The whole time she was just watching him put in his pin number. When they got to the room Misty gave him a rub down and he was knocked out. She grabbed his watch and his ATM card and was gone.

It was a little after 4 a.m. Misty figured that after she worked the card she would go mingle with the

Pimps and Hoes for a while before she went back to her

room.

Chapter Twelve

VEGAS LIFE

Misty made it back to the room around 6 a.m. with 800 and the Cartier watch. Not her idea of a good night, but she was sure that she would get at least $1500 for the watch so she wasn't really tripping.

When she got in the room she woke Unique up and asked her if she wanted to go get down. She said that she wanted to wait until later. Okay, that's twice, Misty thought to herself. She has one more time. Then she laid down and got some rest.

Misty woke up around ten and Unique was dressed. "Are we going to the nail shop and shopping?"

Unique asked. Misty checked the time and said, "Yeah, we are. Give me a minute. Misty got up and jumped in the shower and got dressed. She made sure to grab her laptop and they were out the door.

They pulled up to the swapmeet and Misty handed Unique some money and said, "Here is $300. There should be a nail shop in there, if not there is one right across the street. Don't be all day. Call me when you are ready." "Ok, but I thought you were coming with me." Unique said. "Girl please, I do not shop at the swapmeet. Besides I have other things to take care of." Misty said then drove off.

Misty went to Starbucks and got a caramel Frappuccino, with a double shot of espresso. She enjoyed her dose of caffeine as she searched the internet for apartments. She found one in Summerlin that sounded like somewhere she pictured herself living, so she went to look at it. It was three bedrooms, two baths, all granite counter tops, a fireplace, a roman tub in the master bathroom, all stainless steel appliances, washer and dryer, and vaulted ceilings. It was $1000 per month, so Misty gave the rent for the first three months and got an immediate move in. Then she went to the Budget Suites on Tropicana and got Unique a spot for a month. She made a few more stops and then headed back to pick up Unique. It was perfect timing.

Unique got in the car with a bunch of black plastic bags. "Let me see your nails." Misty said. Unique held out her hands, they were French tipped, but with a different color of the rainbow on every tip. Her toes were the same. "Cute" Misty said then, handed her a bag and said, "Put this on." It was a long, straight, jet black wig. "Ooooh, this is nice." Unique said as she took the old one off and put it on. "It looks hella good on you." Misty said. "Thank you." Unique replied. "So are you ready to go get down and try out your new look or are you gon wait until later?" Misty asked. "I will wait until later." Unique said.

And that is three, Misty thought. "Unique I have given you three chances to make the right decision and all three times you have chosen to wait instead of work. No more being nice, you no longer have a choice. You are going to get down, stay down and remain down. You have no quota, you are just going to work and keep working. Your problem is that you want to do the bare

minimum and wait for somebody to do something for

you instead of taking care of yourself. And I will tell you

right now, I am not taking care of no grown ass woman,

you can not pay me to be your mother. The room that

you slept in last night is damn there $1000 per night and

you have made all together $1010, and you seem to

think that is ok. For now on I will not be asking you what

you wanna do I will be telling you what you are going to

do. It is three o' clock. I am about to drop you off on the

track and I will be back at eleven to break you and drop

you off on the strip." Misty said. "Misty are you mad at

me?" Unique asked. "No, I have no reason to be mad at

you. I just don't deal with lazy bitches. If you wanna fuck

wit me then get like me. When you start taking your

money as seriously as I take mines then we can be partners, until then all I will do is put you down and break you." Misty said. "Ok, I understand. Can I at least get something to eat before you drop me off?" Unique said. "Do you have any condoms?" Misty asked. "Yes, I have one more." Unique replied. "Ok, good. When you catch your first trick, get another pack of condoms, and then get something to eat on the track. Don't spend no more than $20." Misty said as she was pulling into the gas station on the track. She got some gas and Unique went to work.

Thinking about how much money she had left, Misty knew that she had to get on the grind her damn self. But first she needed a drink and a plan. She went back to her room where she could drink in peace and get her thoughts together. At that moment Misty knew three things for sure. The first was that she needed to get some real money real fast. The second was that she should have come alone because she did not like feeling responsible for someone that she could really care less about. And the third thing was that she was lonely.

Then money problem, she was sure would be solved later in the evening. As far as Unique, she would just keep her down until she either bossed up or chose up. The third issue was tricky, because every man that she dealt with wanted more than just a casual encounter every now and then. And for some odd reason every time she had sex with a Pimp she ended up choosing up during sex. She figured that everything would work itself out, and decided to get some rest for the evening.

She woke up around nine and got dressed for the night. She picked up Unique. She had $540 on her. Misty pulled into the Budget Suites and handed Unique a key, "Here your room is number 127 in the G building. All of your things are in there. I will be back in thirty minutes so get fresh and get dressed. And be ready." Misty said.

45 minutes later they were pulling into the Luxor. "Ok, Unique here is $100 for front money. Work the bars like I taught you in the hotels back at home. If you do not catch within an hour, then move to the next casino within walking distance. I will call you at 6 a.m. to see where you are at and pick you up." Misty instructed. "Ok, but I thought that I was working with you tonight."

Unique said. "Not yet." Was all Misty said. Misty decided to go back to Caesars and start her night there. Two hours later she was dropping off $850 in her room and heading elsewhere, on foot.

For the first time Misty felt kind of intimidated by her surroundings, but you couldn't tell by looking at her. She wore a black and white satin dress, that came up around her neck and formed a v that her cleavage tastefully popped out of. It fitted her waist and began to flare at her hips, then went down to about three inches above her knees. She had on a pair of 6" Jimmy Choo stilettos, and a black clutch. Her hair was flowing down her open back. Her makeup was light and flawless, and her lips were glossed to perfection. She gave off sex appeal and confidence as she glided down the strip.

She decided to try her luck at the Flamingo. She walked around and scoped until she spotted her mark at a high limit black jack table. Thirty minutes later they were having a drink at the bar.

And three hours later she was walking out of his room with $1200 and a promise of another $1200 the following night. She decided to call it a night and head back to Caesars. "I see you decided to come to Vegas and play with the big boys." Misty had a knack for remembering voices so she knew exactly who it was. She didn't turn around when she responded. "In case you haven't done your research, I have been playing with the big boys. It's nice of you to finally join us." Misty knew that Lil Giz had been playing with the big boys long before she was, but she had to give him a hard time. "Oh, I have done my research and it told me that you need a real nigga in ya life. So when you are ready you know how to find me." Lil Giz, said in a suave, sexy voice that sent chills up her spine. She shook off the feeling and said, "Nigga leave me alone before I call Giz and tell him that you are harassing me." Misty said, letting the hood chick step out for just a moment. "You haven't seen harassment yet, when I harass you trust me you'll know it. Anyways, Giz called me. He knows where you need to be and as soon as you realize it you will be a lot better off." He shot her a wink and walked away.

I am going to cuss Giz out, she thought to herself. Checking her phone to see what time it was, she decided to call and check on Unique. "What's up Ma, how is your night going?" Misty asked. "I only got one trick for $300." Unique said. "Wow ok. Take a taxi back to your room, drop off the money, change into track clothes, and be down no later than 7. Get you something to eat after you catch your first date. I will check on you at 2." Misty hung up.

"Those were some pretty good instructions there. I couldn't have given them better myself." Misty heard coming from a voice in her left ear. "Why do you mutha fuckas do that shit?" The hood came all of the way out as she swirled around with attitude.

She was facing one of the finest pimps that she ever seen. He stood about 5'11", maybe 190lbs., a shade lighter than her with perfect skin, light brown eyes, and immaculately dressed in a red button down with a white collar and cuffs, white slacks, and red gators.

"Whoa, lil mama, what mutha fuckas are you referring to?" He asked. "Pimps, are the mutha fuckas that I am referring to. Why do all of you feel like you have the right to just intrude in a woman's space just because you are interested in her? The least you can do is introduce yourself before you go whispering shit in people's ear." Misty snapped and then continued on her way. "Ok, well wait a minute."

He said as he gently grabbed her arm and stepped in front of her. He reached out his hand and said, "The name is SinFul, and I would love to converse with you for a while if you have the time."

His hands are so soft and he smells as good as he looks. Misty thought to herself. She wondered if he could see the lust in her eyes. "Catchy name, mines is Misty. And I was actually about to go enjoy the last few hours of my suite. So no, I do not have time. You have a good morning." Misty said. Misty knew good and well that she wanted to converse with him. But she really wanted to relax and she had to secure her money before she invited him up to her room. "On second thought, how about if I call you in an hour. Would you like to join me for breakfast in my suite?" She asked. "That would be wonderful." He said with a perfect smile. They exchanged business cards and Misty went up to her room and he went to the bar.

Misty jumped into the shower and changed into

her favorite basketball shorts and wife beater. She got

all of her money together except for $500 that she put

in her purse. She called down to valet and asked them

to pull her car up so that she wouldn't be standing there

waiting. She slipped right by the bar without him

noticing and to the valet to secure her money in her car.

She tipped the valet $20 and then went back in.

"Are you ready for breakfast, Sir?" Misty

whispered in SinFul's ear as she crept up behind him.

"You seem to pick up Pimpin's techniques very well,

young lady." He said amusingly. "It would seem that

way. Are you ready, because I am starving." Misty said.

"I am following you. Nice get up by the way. I almost

didn't notice you as you passed by the bar the first

time." He winked as he got up from the barstool.

"Thank you, the dress and heels are how I get money, this is how I relax. And It is good to know that you stay aware of your surroundings." Misty said. They then headed up to the room.

Chapter Thirteen

SINFUL, LUSTFUL INTENTIONS

"This is a nice suite. You have fine taste. So tell me why you don't have folks." SinFul said. "Thank you. And the answer to your question is because I am grown and fully capable of instructing and guiding myself. I've tried to choose up for the companionship, but it never works." Misty said as she grabbed the room service menu and handed it to him. "I know what I want already. Not to rush you, but I am starving." Misty said. "Let's make it easy. I will just have what you're having." He said as he handed her the menu back. "Do you mind if I get comfortable?" He asked as he began to unbutton his shirt.

Misty almost choked on her words as she was

ordering two seafood omelettes, when she looked up and seen him standing there in his wife beater. She cursed herself for not wearing something sexy and seductive. At that moment there was no limit to the things that she wanted to do to him. But oh well she thought, he doesn't seem like the type to fuck before he gets paid anyway. She dismissed the thought.

"It's going to be thirty to forty-five minutes. Do you smoke?" Misty said when she hung up the phone. "Yes, I actually do." He said. "What do you drink? I have Remy, but I can order something different if you would like." Misty said. "Remy is perfect. Who were you instructing earlier? It doesn't seem like two people are staying in this room." He asked as he was looking around. "Not that it really matters. But since you asked,

I am here because I felt like I deserved this for the weekend and I can afford it. And she can't afford it so she isn't here. As simple as that." Misty said.

"Let's cut the chase Ma. Why did you invite me up here?" SinFul asked in a subtle yet dominant voice. Misty handed him his drink, sipped hers, lit the blunt, and said, "I was bored. Pimps are usually interesting, and you made yourself available." Misty could tell that he did not like the answer that she gave, but he controlled himself because he really wanted to have her.

He stood up and walked over to Misty, who was curled up on the couch. "The only reason that I haven't broke you yet is because I like your style and I think that we will get along a lot better if I allow you to break yourself when you get ready to. But not for one minute should you think that you are going to amuse yourself with my company and not pay for it. Are you understanding me?" SinFul said in a somewhat evil voice.

For a moment Misty was taken in by his dominance and sexiness. And if she had already been settled in with a nice amount of money, the hoe in her would have won this battle. She looked up at him with those big hazel eyes and he thought that he had her, then she said, "The only reason that you haven't broke me is because I haven't broke myself, and if I was going to do it, then it would have already been done. And if you think for one minute that you are going to intimidate me into doing so then you have me sadly mistaken for one of these punk bitches out here. Now I think that it would be best if you left before we bump heads any further." Misty said with a lot of attitude.

In one swift movement SinFul pushed the table back and lifted Misty to her feet, and as close to him as he could possibly get her. His face was in hers and he said, "I don't know what kind of pimps you have been running into, but that tough girl act doesn't do anything but make me want you more. And the more that I want you the harder I go. And trust me, I can go harder than you have ever imagined possible........." "Knock, knock, knock, room service." He released her from his grip of fury and said, "Get the door so that we can enjoy our breakfast."

Misty wanted to say fuck that breakfast. In

between her legs was on fire and she wanted SinFul to put the fire out. But she did as she was told. She grabbed her purse, answered the door, and paid for their food.

While they were eating neither of them said a word. Misty wanted SinFul's dick and SinFul wanted Misty's all. They were both trying to figure out how to get what they wanted. Misty didn't really have the patience. "Look, I wanna fuck you, but I am not ready to choose up with anyone right now. So rather than play these games just let me know how much can I give you to fuck me until check out time?" Misty said in a very businesslike manner.

SinFul raised his eyebrows and tried his hardest not to smile. His hardest was not good enough. He smiled and said, "As pleased as I am to know that you are attracted to me, I am not into selling my swipe. What you can pay for is this pimpin and when the time is right I will give you what you desire and much more."

Misty climbed out of the bed and proceeded to take off her shorts, then her tank top. As she bent over to grab an outfit out of her bag she said, "Oh well, I guess neither one of us will be getting what we want this morning."

Misty could see the bulge in his slacks rising. She thought to herself, "Check." She decided to take this a step further. "Excuse me for a moment, I need to jump in the shower and wet my hair." She said. When she came out of the bathroom she had on nothing but a towel wrapped around her and her hair and body was still dripping wet. She bent over to wrap her dripping hair in another towel, and before she could do it he had her pinned against the wall. She thought to herself, "Mate."

An hour later he was sleep and Misty was waiting for her car in valet. When he woke up there was a note on the pillow next to him.

SinFul,

Thank you for the decent morning. I needed that. I would have stayed but I have business to tend to. Meet me at the bar that you were at this morning at midnight.

Misty oxoxo

Misty waited at the bar, it was 12:15 when SinFul arrived. She waved down the bartender and ordered two double shots of Remy, gave the bartender a hundred and said keep the change. "Miss baller baller. How are you this evening?" SinFul said, obviously impressed by the tip that Misty gave the bartender. "I'm not a baller. I just know that when you take care of your servers they take care of you, and keep you informed." Misty said. "Which let's me know that you know what you're doing out here." Sinful said. "That, I do." Misty said as she handed him a dollar bill. Sinful had a confused look on his face. "The rest is in the machine that you are sitting in front of. I'll catch you around." Misty said as she got up and walked away.

Knowing that, that particular bar required a

hand payout from the bartender, Misty knew that she had time to get to her car, that she paid the valet to keep in the front, and be gone.

SinFul looked at the machine, it said $999.00. He pushed the "cash out" button. He was pissed when the "Hand Payout Required" signal flashed across the screen. By the time he made it out to the valet, she was gone. He figured he would see her around sooner or later.

Chapter Fourteen

PERFECT TIMING

"Hey you, I ain't spoke to you in forever. What's going on?" Misty said as she answered a call from Frustrated.

Frustrated was a pimp that Misty met a few years back. She never actually chose up with him but they manage to stay in touch. And despite her broken promises of getting to him they actually developed a very good friendship.

"Not much, just dealing with these weirdo ass bitches. Waiting for you to stop playing and come home." He said in a playful tone. "Stop waiting and come get me then. Just keep me away from those wierd ass hoes, I don't play well with idiots." Misty said. "Which makes me wonder, how the fuck you been playing with yourself for so long……" They both laughed. "Ha, ha, ha, you got jokes today." Misty said.

"You know I'm just playing. You ain't no idiot. But bitch you are lost and confused, and you know it. So what adventure are you on now?" Frustrated asked.

"Let's see, shit. Where do I start? I got like five or six pimps that might, very well attempt to do something to me if they see me because I left them. I've been in Vegas for about a month, adding to the list. Oh, and I got a bitch whose folks got shot. She is dumb as fuck and doesn't have a clue what to do. You can have her if you want. She listens very well." Misty said in almost one breath. "Bitch, you're crazy. One of those niggaz is gon shoot you if you don't stop playing." He said. "Not if I get to my piece first they won't. It ain't my fault these niggaz don't know how to keep me." Misty said. "That ain't the problem. The problem is that you don't wanna be kept." Frustrated replied. "Yeah, yeah, yeah. Let's not get into my psychological issues today. When are you going to come see me? It's been too long." Misty said, trying to avoid a conversation about what she needed because she knew that he was right.

"I don't know yet. I have to get these hoes under control first. I got a real weird bunch right now." He said. "Do you want one more?" Misty asked. "Yeah, you finally ready to come home?" He replied. "You wish I was, naw you can have this bitch. But you have to come get her, that way I get to see you. She a cool bitch though, but all I do is send her and break her. I am sure that she is going to choose up any day now. Shit, I wish she would hurry the fuck up cuz I ain't got the patience. I ain't no damn Pimp. But yeah, she works slow but she stays down. I keep her down between sixteen and twenty hours a day and she makes between $800 and

$1200. It's up to you. If you want her, then come get her." Misty explained. "Just send the bitch to me. I can't leave here right now." He said. "Nope, I wanna see you, so come get her." Misty said stubbornly. "That's your problem. You always wanna do shit your way." He said. "I know, come get me and change that, then." Misty said playfully. "Let me answer this call Imma hit you back later." Frustrated said. "Ok, talk to you later." Misty said. It might be another six months before they speak again. That is how they were.

Out of every pimp that Misty has ever came across Frustrated was the only one that she allowed herself to be completely real with. So even though she never actually chose up with him he had an intimate knowledge of her. Sometimes she thought that he knew her better than she knew herself. She knew that they would be good together but she had too much respect for him and she cherished their friendship too much to risk messing up and losing him.

It was Friday night, close to 10pm. Misty decided to start out at the Mirage. It was slow so she walked down towards Caesars Palace.

Out of nowhere someone snatched her from behind by her hair. She would have fell but he kept her standing by her hair. Within seconds she was against the wall and staring in the face of a pimp named Chaos that she left a while back.

Chaos was about 5'9", kind of chunky, light skinned, with braids. She fucked with him a couple of years back for a month. When she left him he had his bitches try to fight her. Then he chased her and one of her tricks through Hollywood at high speed.

"Are you fuckin kidding me. Nigga get yo mutha fuckin hands off of me!" Misty said in an irritated voice. "Bitch, you gon break yoself tonight!" Chaos said. "I ain't breakin a mutha fuckin thing, and if I was it wouldn't be ta yo weird ass..........." Misty said.

Out of nowhere they both heard, "A Cuzz, ain't that Giz cousin Misty over there?"

Misty knew that voice anywhere. It was Baby Giz and she was damn glad to hear him, because she didn't know how she was going to get out of this situation without getting beat up. and let Baby Giz and Lil Giz finish him off.

It startled Chaos and he turned around. When he turned around Misty pushed him back the stuck him with a quick two piece. One to the jaw and another to the chin. Then she stood back "That nigga was bout to fuck you up, Cuzz!" Baby Giz exclaimed. "Yeah, I know and I just would have had to take it cuzz I ain't got no money on me to give the nigga, and no pistol to shoot the nigga." Misty said as she was looking at her hand that was swelling up.

"Baby, it looks like you might need to take the night off and tend to that hand." Lil Giz said. "Only if you gon take the night off with me." Misty said in a sweet voice. "That sounds like it might be a plan. Where we going" Lil Giz replied. "My spot is on Flamingo and Fort

Apache. Baby Giz, you coming I got food, drinks, extra rooms, whatever you need." Misty said. "Let's go!" Baby Giz said.

"When did you get a spot? Everybody is referring to you as, 'the bitch that stays at Ceasars'?" Lil Giz asked. "I got a spot the second day I was out here. And who is everybody and why are they referring to me" Misty said in a feisty tone. "You know the streets talk, especially when a sexy mutha fucka like you starts moving around. And you better stop playin wit pimps before you are known as the faggot at Caesars." Lil Giz said, knowing that would get a rise out of her.

"Fuck these niggaz. I don't give a fuck about what they say about me. They just mad cuz they can't have me. I can't stand pimps, them niggaz gossip like bitches. The only thing good that some of them have is dick. That's why I fuck em, throw em a rack and be gon before they wake up. They ain't nothing but fuck boys." Misty said with a major attitude. The hood chick was all the way in effect now. Lil Giz was amused.

"So what are you saying about me? I'm a pimp." Lil Giz said. "You a real nigga. Pimpin is just something that you do. And from what I hear it aint the only thing." Misty said. "So you have been inquiring about me. That's a good thing. So tell me baby, what have you heard?" Lil Giz replied. Misty smiled. "I know enough to know that if any nigga had a chance to have me that they would have to compare to you." She said.

"Ok, so do you want me to take you to your car so y'all can follow me or are we all riding in my car"

Misty asked as her car pulled up. "I'm leaving my car for my bitch, so she can get home. That way I can, uumm, tend to your hand." He said in a suave voice that had Misty moist instantaneously. "Tend to my hand, huh. Is that all you will be tending to?" Misty asked. "I wouldn't want you thinking of me as one of those 'fuck boys' so yeah, that is all I will be tending to tonight." Lil Giz said.

"I'm just gon stay out here, Cuzz. Y'all drop me off at Bill's." Baby Giz said. "Are you sure Bruh Bruh" Lil Giz asked. "Yeah, cuzz y'all on some other shit. And I'm not about to be sitting there bored." Baby Giz replied. "Aiight, your call." Lil Giz said.

When they got back to Misty's she went straight to the back and grabbed the first aid kit. Lil Giz found a bottle of Remy and two glasses and poured them a drink. "I see that you have made yourself at home." Misty said as she returned wearing some b-ball shorts and a tank top, with the first aid kit in hand.

He patted the seat next to him on the sofa. "Have a seat and let me look at that hand Mrs. Tyson." He said. "Ha, ha, ha." Misty said sarcastically playful.

After he wrapped up her hand they talked and laughed for a while. Then he led her to her room and just held her. As Misty laid there she was amazed at how good it felt to be in his arms. How good it felt to be cared for. How good it felt to be treated like a lady and a baby at the same time. They both fell asleep.

IS TODAY THE CHOSEN DAY

Misty's alarm went off at 6am. Still in his arms Misty grabbed her phone, stopped the alarm from going off and called Unique.

"Where you at Unique?" Misty asked. "I am at the Wynn." Unique said. "Alright catch a taxi back to your room and get some rest. I'm gon pick you up around 11 or 12 and take you shopping. How much do you got?" Misty said. "I haven't broke yet." Unique said.

Misty could tell that she was about to cry. "Alright, don't trip. We all have bad nights. What you do is instead of going to get some rest go to Tropicana and call me when you get five. If it's early enough then we'll still go shopping. If not then we will go tomorrow. Text me and let me know when you are down." Misty said.

"But I don't have any money." Unique said as she started crying. "Look, I don't do that crying shit and I don't deal with it either. In your room on the very top shelf over the cups it's some money. Use only what you need for the taxi. I'll talk to you later." Misty hung up.

When Misty hung up she could feel Lil Giz looking at her. "You are full of surprises. Who was that?" He said. "This lil bitch that I brought out here. Do you want her?" Misty replied. "I'll take her, but I want you. Are you ready to stop playin yet?" Lil Giz said.

"How did I know that was coming? When I am ready

you will know. I still have a few things that I need to do

on my own. Would you like some breakfast?" Misty

said. "Breakfast would be nice, but not yet. It's too

early. Lay back down." Lil Giz said as he pulled her back

close to him.

Misty wanted to get up because she was scared

of how good it felt to be in his arms. The only two men

in her life that showed her affection and concern were

her dad and Giz, and she figured that is what they were

supposed to do. But he had no obligation to her, so why

was he giving her this treatment. She wondered if it was

genuine or if this is what he did to every bitch.

"I can't sleep. I'm getting up. Breakfast will be

ready in about thirty minutes." Misty said as she was climbing out of bed. "You wake up too damn early for me." Lil Giz said as he walked into the kitchen. "Don't nothing come to a sleeper but a dream and I like reality."Misty said.

"Here you go Sir, one steak and potato omelette." Misty handed him his plate. "Thank you Ma. It smells good. Where's your plate?" He replied. "Oh, I don't eat breakfast. I'm gon run to Starbucks real quick. Enjoy your breakfast, I'll be right back." She said as she was walking out the door.

Lil Giz wondered why the hell this woman was single. Despite her stubbornness, there was a way to get through to her. Little did he know he had already gotten through to her.

"Did you enjoy your breakfast?" Misty asked as she walked through the door. "Of course I did. Thank you, Baby." He said as he kissed her on the cheek. "You're welcomed. What time would you like me to take you home?" She asked. "Whenever you're ready, I'm on your time. I don't have anything to do." He said

"Alright well I am about to do something on the internet, while I enjoy my coffee. Then I will get dressed and we can go, because unlike you, I have things to do." Misty said. "Do you ever sit still? Lil Giz asked. "I'll sit still either when I am satisfied or when I die. Whichever comes first." Misty snapped back.

She checked her phone and she had a text from Frustrated. "On my way. Be there around noon. The bitch betta be worth it and you betta have some money and a home cooked meal waiting for me."

Misty felt herself get excited. She hadn't seen him in three years. She texted back a smiley face. It was only 8:30 so she had time to get prepared.

"So what's up wit this bitch you got?" Lil Giz asked. "Forget about her. Somebody is on their way to come get her as we speak. I just got the message." Misty said. "Fuck it. Just let me know when you are ready. I'm about to go lay down until it's time to go." He said. "Well, it won't be long." She said.

An hour later she was dropping him off and heading to the grocery store. Her phone rang and Y.T.'s picture popped on her screen. "Hey, you're my friend again?" Misty said when she answered. "Bitch, you

know you gon always be my nigga. What are you doing?
I heard that you was in Vegas makin niggaz look bad."
Y.T. said. "These niggaz make themselves look bad. And
why do mutha fuckas insist on having my name in they
mouth?" Misty said. "I don't know, maybe cuz all you do
is run around doing faggot shit. Anyways, what are you
doing at 8:15 tonight? I need you to pick me up from
the airport. And I need you to book me a room, I don't
really give a fuck where." Y.T. said. "Don't trip, I will be
there and your room will be ready. Do you need a
rental?" Misty said. "My nigga, I knew you would come
through. Don't worry about the rental." Y.T. said.
"Alright, I'll see you when you get here." Misty hung up.

She wondered what tricks he had up his sleeves.
Y.T. was always up to something. She dismissed it and

called Caesar's to book his room, and paid for it for two nights. She would go put a bottle of Remy on the bed later on.

It was going on 10, she figured that she'd better hurry and get things ready for Frustrated. Then her phone rang again. This is why I keep my phone on silent, she thought. She didn't recognize the number.

"Hello." She answered. "Why haven't you called?" The voice on the other end said. She didn't catch the voice. "I might have an answer to that, if I knew who this was." She replied. "Oh, you don't know my voice anymore?" He said. "What do you want Scrappe?" She said. "I wanna know why my bitch hasn't called me in over a month." He said. "I stopped being yo bitch the day I left." Misty said. "As far as I'm concerned, you are still my bitch. Ain't nobody served me." He said. "And ain't nobody served any other nigga I left either. I keep tellin you niggaz that hoeing is what I do it is not who I am. So, I don't give a fuck about those dumb ass rules of the game. Now, what did you call me for cuz I'm busy?" Misty snapped through the phone. "I'm in Vegas. Where are you?" He said. "You being in Vegas has nothing to do with me. I am at home enjoying my life, but like I said I'm busy. Good bye." She hung up.

What the fuck is going on? Why did all these niggaz pick today to come out here? I have to figure something out and I have to do it quick. Frustrated is gon wanna go on the strip. Y.T. is gon be on the strip. And I don't know where the fuck Scrappe is going to be. The next few days are going to be interesting.

LIGHTS OUT

Misty and Frustrated sat there and talked, laughed, ate, and drank for a few hours. Then her phone rang. "This is the bitch right here." She said to Frustrated.

"Hey Unique, you got five yet?" Misty asked. "I got six and I am very tired." Unique said. "Alright, well go back to the room, take a bath, and get some rest. It is

3:00 now be up and ready for the strip at 9:00. And make sure that your place is spotless because I might bring someone there." Misty hung up.

She looked at Frustrated and said, "whatever you want her to do from this point on is on you. She doesn't do good on the strip. She's a track star. I just send her out there for playtime, but she doesn't know that though." Misty said. "Bitch you are truly a cold piece of work. I need to pimp on you like you pimp on that bitch. You lucky I like you." Frustrated said. "Yeah, yeah. Well, her room is up at the end of the week. I don't know how long you plan on being out here but after tonight you gon have to stay over there with her because for some reason everybody chose today to come to Vegas. So, I am going to be busy pissing people off, mostly pimps. But it was great seeing you and you are welcomed for the bitch." Misty said. "Damn, you been rushing me out here and now you rushing me to leave. You just do me any kind of way. Naw, I'm leaving in a few hours anyway. I got to get back before these bitches burn my house down or some other weird shit." He said. "Well shit, we can go to the bitch right now." Misty said. "Let's go. I'll follow you." Frustrated said. "Ok, well I figured that I will tell her to open the door for you and you work your magic from there. She has $600 on her and there is 250 in the emergency stash." Misty said. "You come in, introduce me, and leave the rest up to me." He said. "Ok, that will work." She said.

Two hours later Frustrated and Unique were on the highway and Misty was at home getting dressed and prepared for the evening. She was glad that she didn't have the extra responsibility of Unique anymore.

She had just enough time to roll a blunt and get a bottle of Remy before it was time to pick Y.T. up from the airport. When he got in the car she handed him a styrofoam cup, a blunt, and a lighter.

"Here you go. I'm sure that you need it after dealing with all of the airport bullshit." She said. "You always treat a nigga right. But bitch you know that this is why all of these niggaz trip out when you leave them." Y.T. said. "Most of these niggaz don't get this treatment. You are of a very select few. Consider yourself special." Misty said. "Shut up bitch. You still a faggot. Where you book my room at?" He said. "You are such an asshole, and that's why I love you. I got it at

Caesars. I paid for the first two nights and put $500 on it so that you can order room service. After that it's up to you. How long are you going to be here?" Misty said. "That's what's up my nigga, good lookin. You fuckin wit me while I am here? I'm not sure how long yet. And what happened to your hand?" He said. "I'm gon fuck wit you off and on. You know I be movin and shakin. And this happened last night. Some weirdo nigga that I left a while back snatched me up and I two pieced 'em then my home boys took over." Misty explained. "That's crazy." Was all he said.

When they got out of the car in valet Misty gave the attendant a twenty and said, "Keep it up front please." "Yes, Ms. Green." He said. As soon as they walked through the entrance Misty saw SinFul. Her heart dropped. She and Y.T. made it to the registration desk before SinFul noticed her. She seen him sitting there patiently waiting for her. As they were walking off from the desk she saw him walking their way.

"Y.T. please act like I'm your bitch." Misty pleaded. Y.T. was about to ask her what she was talking about, but then he seen SinFul walking up to him. "I should let this nigga fuck you up. Bitch, you probably deserve it." Y.T. said. Misty did not say a word. She knew that Y.T. meant what he said. She just put her head down.

"Say P, how you doing? The name is SinFul and I got issues wit this bitch right here." SinFul said as he walked up. "Y.T. mane. Check this out, whatever issues you had wit the bitch was before I got 'er so I ain't got nothing to do wit that. But the bitch is mines now, so you gon have to let that shit go." Y.T. said.

Misty was relieved because she had a feeling that Y.T. was gon do some vengeful shit.

"But, I'll tell you what we can do P." Y.T. said. Misty knew that she thought too soon. "You can slap this bitch a few times, cuz I am sure that she deserves it. If that makes you feel better." Y.T. said.

SinFul seemed to be pondering the idea, but Misty wasn't having it. "And if you put yo mutha fuckin hands on me the coroner will be picking you up off of this mutha fuckin casino floor. I paid you for yo sorry ass dick so you need to be happy." Misty snapped. Then she turned to Y.T., "And nigga you got me fucked up......."

"SMACK" Y.T. slapped the rest of the words right out of her mouth. "Now, bitch go up to the room and wait for me to get up there." Y.T. said.

Misty was more embarrassed than anything. But she knew that reputation was everything that a pimp had so the moment that she turned to disrespect him Y.T. had no other choice. So she handed him a key and without a single word she walked off.

"Bitch, have you lost your mind?" Y.T. said as soon as he walked into the room. "Y.T. don't go there with me. You know damn well that I was not about to let that nigga put his mutha fuckin hands on me." She snapped. "Bitch, I know that. I don't give a fuck about what you said to dat nigga. But bitch don't ever think that you gon talk to me like one of these fuck boys dat you be playin wit." He said as he lit a blunt. "I know,

Y.T., my bad. I apologize. Misty said. "And bitch how da

fuck was you gon manage to kill dat nigga if he did

decide to slap yo ass, like I did?" Y.T. asked. "Y.T. I stay

heated." Misty said. "Yeah ok, yo ass betta slow down

and be careful, bitch." He said. "Shit, that's why I carry

it, to stay careful. But shit it's already 10. Let me go

make this money back that I spent on your room. I

should be done by like 1 or 2 and I will hit you up and

come fuck wit cha." Misty said. "Alright my nigga, I'll be

on the strip somewhere harassin a prostitute." He said.

"Don't harass, nigga knock." She said as she was walking

out the door.

She checked her phone and had eight missed

calls from Scrappe and one from Lil Giz. She ignored

Scrappe and called Lil Giz back. "What's good Mama? How's your hand?" He said when he answered the phone. "It's cool. I still have it wrapped in your magic bandage. It does nothing for my outfit though. Where you at wit it?" Misty replied. "I'm down at my lil bar havin a drink before I hit the strip and get to work. You gettin out tonight?" Lil Giz said. "I'm already out. I'm gon be out of the way tonight because ya boy Scrappe is out here and I am sure that it is not going to be nice if he catches up wit me." Misty said. "Yeah, I know. He hit me up earlier, but he didn't say anything about you though. But if I see him I will hit you up and let you know where not to go." Lil Giz said. "Aiight, G safe. I'll talk to you later." Misty said. "Misty" Lil Giz said. "Yes, Lil Giz." She replied. "You know all you gotta do is fuck wit me and you ain't gotta worry about none of these niggaz, right." He said. "When I do fuck wit you, it definitely won't be to get away from another nigga." She said and then hung up.

Just as she hung up she saw the valet pulling up with her car. And right behind it was Scrappe with his door already opened and one foot out of the car, looking over the hood at her. Knowing that her pride would not allow her to cause a scene, he handed the valet his keys and got in her passenger seat. Not knowing what else to do she dialed Lil Giz phone number as she was getting in the car so that he would hear what was going on.

"What do you want Scrappe?" She asked. He said nothing. Then out of nowhere he backhanded her.

She took a deep breath and kept driving. "Can we go have a drink and talk about this before it gets out of control?" She asked. He backhanded her again. They were almost to the bar. She hoped that they made it there before he went ballistic or before she did.

The bar was behind Bill's and across the street from Bally's. They were at the light waiting to make a U-turn. She could see Lil Giz standing outside shaking his head.

"Bitch, you ain't been wantin to talk. I didn't come out here to talk. I warned you about playin wit me. But yeah, let's get a drink." Scrappe said.

As soon as she parked she seen Lil Giz walking up to the car, then she felt a surge of pain on the right side of her face, and a dizzy feeling, then nothing.

"Oh my gosh. Why am I in so much pain? Why are you driving my car? And where are we going?" She said as she woke up. "Just relax, Mama. I'm taking you home. Don't worry I remember the way." Lil Giz said.

Remembering what happened Misty said, "Oh my gosh, I am so sorry for putting you in this. I know that's your homeboy." "Don't worry about it. Cuzz wasn't trippin on me. He got out of the car sayin that you are lucky that Giz is yo cousin. Baby Giz took him into the bar and I tended to you. You been out for like five minutes." He said. "That's the first time that I have been knocked out. Cuzz hits hella hard." She said. "Well you better slow down. This is the second night in a row that I saved you. I might not be there next time." He said. "It's not my fault that these niggaz don't know how to let go. Besides, take your left hand and feel up under that seat. I gave that nigga a pass before he gave me one. And I guarantee that he knows that." Misty said.

"Ok, well I guess we will be at your place for another night." Lil Giz said. "Actually, no we're not. Just let me pack a duffle bag and I will drop you back off. I have other plans for myself tonight. But I really do appreciate you being there for me." Misty said.

She grabbed enough clothes for a week and enough money for two weeks and they were out of there. Misty had also grabbed an extra $1500 for Lil Giz. When she dropped him off she got out of the car and gave him a hug a whispered in his ear, "One day we might make each other happy. But for now, thank you."

She slipped the money into his shirt pocket, gave him a kiss on the cheek, jumped back into the car and headed back up to Ceasars. She was ready for a couple of days with Y.T. and a week of relaxation.

ONCE AGAIN, LIL GIZ TO THE

RESCUE

"Damn, I needed that." Misty said to herself as

she walked through her door. She poured herself a

drink, rolled a blunt, then laid on her sofa and enjoyed the comforts of her home that she hadn't seen in a week. She got up a few hours later, did some light cleaning, and cut up some fresh fruit. "I guess I'll get back out to work tonight." She said to herself.

She decided to wear one of the outfits that she just got. A white leather playboy mini skirt and jacket, a black halter top, and 6" stiletto, knee high, platform boots. She took a look in the mirror and said, "Oh yeah, I'm playing the Hard Rock and the Palms tonight."

Misty went to the Palms first. As soon as she was walking in a gentleman that was walking out turned around and slid his arm under hers. "I think that tonight is my lucky night." He said. "It definitely could be as long as it is my lucky night as well. But may I ask what makes you so lucky tonight?" Misty said. "I was just about to go out and look for the woman of my dreams and as I was walking out she was walking in." He said. "And in your dreams what do you and this woman do?" Misty asked. "How about we go to my room and I will show you." He said. "I thought that's where we were headed." Misty said.

Three hours later she was walking out of the palms with $1500 and a Rolex. And she didn't even have to steal it. She asked for it and he gave it to her. She was quite pleased.

Now it was time for the Hard Rock. Misty figured that she would have a few drinks before she went up to a room with anyone. She figured wrong, 45 minutes later she was leaving there with $500. She expected more but she didn't want to be greedy. At this point Misty figured that she would just mingle and have fun. If something happened then it did and if not then so be it.

She parked at Bally's then crossed over towards Bill's. The strip was pretty busy and the pimps and hoes were out in full effect. All with one thing in mind, getting money. Misty loved it. And she loved it even more that she got hers.

"I'm not gon watch yo sexy ass for too much longer. I'm trying to be nice and let you come on your own. But then you come out lookin like this it gives a pimp no choice but to sweat cha." Misty heard in her right ear. "Lil Giz you can sweat me from here to da Garr and you still have no choice but to let me come on my own. What are you drinking tonight? My treat." Misty said as she walked into the Flamingo. "If you was any other bitch, I'll break you. You know dat right?" He said.

She handed the bartender a hundred and said, "a double shot of Remy with a twist of lime on ice and a double shot of Patron straight. Keep the change." Then she turned to Lil Giz and said, "I hope that you are not going easy on me because of Giz, cuzz that takes the fun out of it." They both grabbed their drinks. "It has nothing to do with Giz. But when I do decide to break you or make you break yo'self it will be for everything and not just what's in yo purse. You remember that." He kissed her on the cheek. "Thank you for the drink. Now go put some more in that stash for Daddy." He walked away and left Misty standing there with her panties moist. "Damn that nigga is sexy as fuck." Misty said to herself as she sipped her drink.

She decided to head down to the Mirage. As soon as she walked in a weird looking black guy with green eyes walked up to her, flashed his badge, and said, "Come with me." "Hold up! For what?" Misty said as she snatched her arm out of his grip and stopped walking. "For loitering with the intent of prostitution, and we can add resisting arrest if you keep up with the attitude." He said. "First of all I just walked in here, so I wasn't loitering anywhere." Misty snapped. "Save it for court. As of now you are going to jail." He said.

Misty was pissed, but she knew that it was in her best interest to not say anything more. She cursed herself for not having a bail bonds and an attorney already paid and ready to come get her.

After she was booked she called Lil Giz. She knew that she had to stop calling him to save her. But she was in jail and this was not the time to stop. "Well, well, well if it isn't my independent, renegade hoe calling me, a pimp that she's not ready to be with, from jail." Lil Giz said when he answered. "Oh my gosh, can you just come get me. My bail is only $1000. Can you bring the whole thing up here and pay it because a bail bonds is going to take entirely too long and if I have to stay in here too much longer with these dumb ass broke bitches I'm gon catch another charge. I will pay you back as soon as I get to my car." Misty said. "I'm not gon play wit you because I don't want you to catch another case. But I am telling you right now that you are gon do more than just pay me back. I'm on my way." Lil Giz said.

"Thank you." Misty said. "Don't thank me yet. You might not wanna thank me when I come get you." He said then hung up.

When she got released he was right there waiting. "Damn Mama, I ain't never seen a bitch walk out of jail lookin as good as you. You even still smell good." He said when she got in the car. "Thank you. My car is parked at Bally's." Misty said. "You'll get to your car when I am ready to take you to it. For now you are with me." He said as he pulled off. "Since you bailed me out you think that you can hold me captive? Where are we going?" Misty asked with an attitude. She did not have the patience to argue with him. "Actually, yes, I do think that. And I know that you like it. We are going to my place." He said. "Why can't we go to my place? I don't like being in another woman's home. Plus I need a shower." Misty said. "No woman lives at my place and I have a shower. And since I know that you love wearing b-ball shorts and wife beaters, I am going to let you wear my favorite pair. Now do me a favor and sit back and relax. There is a blunt in the ashtray and that Rockstar is half Hennessy." He said as he shot her a wink and turned the music up.

She couldn't help but to smile. He seemed to know just what to say and do. And he was proving himself to be very dependable. She wanted so bad to just give in to him completely, but she just wasn't ready. She loved her freedom and she didn't want to hurt or cross him like she did every other nigga that she dealt with. She hadn't seen for herself but she heard stories about him. She also knew the reputation of the Giz name. So she knew that the flip side to the suave, sweet guy that he was showing her was not something that she wanted to see.

When they got to his place he handed her some towels, shorts, and wife beater and said, "Use the bathroom in my room." When she got out of the shower he was sitting on his bed with a drink in his hand. "Your drink is right there. Come sit down and explain to me why you are so stubborn." He said. She grabbed her drink and sat next to him. "I am just not ready to be under instructions again. I gave so much of myself to my turnout folks; and in the end I was left with pain, anger, and a whole lot of game. And now, I am having too much fun on my own." She said. "I see so being snatched up on the strip, knocked out in your own car, and going to jail with no one to call, and not to mention going home to a lonely bed every night is your idea of fun?" He said. "Shit happens, and when I don't wanna go home to my lonely bed I don't." She said because she didn't know what else to say. "Well, when you are ready to stop 'having fun' and live life then I will be waiting. But until then, for now on every time that you get out of pocket wit me I am breaking you for everything out of your purse and your car. As for this moment, let's enjoy it because there will not be another one until you are ready to be mines." He said. Then he took her drink out of her hand and set it on the night stand. Then in one swift movement he laid her down and kissed her like she had never been kissed before.

She felt as if the entire world had stopped as he was exploring her mouth with his tongue.

Then he got up and began undressing. "Clothes off. Everything!" Was all he said. The warmth of his mouth kissing on her neck, then down to her breast, then down her stomach, and to her inner thigh sent her body into an uproar. The way that he handled her, so gently yet so firm made her fight back tears. And he hadn't even entered her yet. He gently guided her head down, and she enthusiastically went where he wanted her to go. She gulped every inch of him inside of her mouth and deep into her throat. She took her time to make sure that her tongue massaged his entire dick. And she didn't stop until he exploded in her mouth and she did not let a drop go to waste. He pulled her up and laid her on her back. His hand slid down between her lips and the wetness made his dick instantly hard again. When he pushed inside of her it was as if he entered another world. Her pussy gripped his dick and held onto it like it had been waiting on him for a lifetime. And she was holding onto him just as tight. He took long, slow, and deep strokes. "Just like that Daddy. Please don't stop." She said. "Ok Baby." He replied. He felt her pussy gripping tighter and tighter with every stroke that he made. He didn't know how much longer that he could hold back. "Cum for Daddy Baby. I'm almost there and I want it in your mouth." He said. "Yes, Daddy." She could barely get the words out. His strokes started getting deeper, harder, and faster, and she got tighter and tighter. Finally she wrapped her legs around him and her entire body tensed up. This made him go even harder and deeper inside of her. He couldn't hold back any longer and he couldn't stop. She felt him explode inside of her and that sent shock waves through her. Her body began to spasm and tremble. He rolled off of her, pulled her close, and they both passed out.

ON THE RUN

Misty reached to grab her phone and realized that she was alone. It was after two. She couldn't understand how she slept so late in a bed that wasn't her own.

"Why did you let me sleep so late?" She said to

Lil Giz when she walked into the living room. He was relaxed with his feet kicked up, watching a movie. "You needed that sleep. As far as I can tell, you don't get nearly enough. As a matter of fact you probably need to lay back down." He said. "No, can you take me to my car. I need to go get an attorney to take care of this case for me." Misty said. "Today is Sunday. You have close to $700 in your purse. So we are going to go to the mall so you can get an outfit. Then I am going to take us to brunch, lunch, or dinner depending on how long it takes at the mall. Then we are going to pick up your car, go back to your place, get drunk, and go to sleep. Then when we wake up you are going to make me one of those amazing omelets and I am going to be on my way. And after that I am going to have a ball getting you out

of pocket and breaking you every time that I see you."
Lil Giz said.

"That all sounds amazing, but the only way that you are going to see me to break me is if you come to Houston. I am out of here as soon as I hire an attorney tomorrow, and that will be right after I cook your omelet. Now are you ready to go because I need my Starbucks in the next few minutes or I am going to turn into a super bitch." Misty said "In case you haven't noticed you surpassed super bitch a long time ago. But yeah, I'm ready, let's go. Houston, huh?" Lil Giz replied. "Yes, Houston. I need shoes and socks." Misty said. "Top drawer on the right and the Jordan slippers in the closet. Why Houston?" He said. "Because it's fun. I loved it when I lived out there. And I won't have to fight myself about choosing you." Misty said. "Why fight? Why not just choose? We can go to Houston together." Lil Giz said. "Because I am not ready. When I am I will be back. Come on let's go." Misty said. "I ain't never ran across a bitch like you. Why are you so elusive? You just gon make a nigga go hard on you." He said "And you never will because I am a one of a kind. And I am not elusive, I am just not ready. And you can go as hard as the breath in your body allows you to and I will still not break until I am good and ready to." She replied.

They had one of the nicest days and evenings that Misty has had in years. She missed this part of life. The part that wasn't all about making money. A part of her wanted to be his so bad, but a bigger part was terrified of being hurt. She already felt way too deeply about him.

"I'll be back in a few weeks or so. Here is the key to my apartment, just in case. I am going to drive to Gardena first and bring Giz back his car and I will buy one when I get to Houston. I will call you every few days or so just to say hi, if that is ok with you." Misty said. "You can call me whenever you get ready to. You just be careful, ok." He said. "I'll be careful, Daddy. I promise." She said. "You better be. And try not to make nobody kill you. No makin niggaz fall in love wit you. That shit is dangerous." He said. Misty giggled, "I'll try not to." They kissed and he left.

Lil Giz did not feel right about letting her leave, but he knew that her mind was made up and he could not change it.

When she made it back to Gardena and pulled up at Giz house Scrappe's 745 was in the driveway. "Oh my gosh, I do not feel like dealing wit this nigga." Misty said to herself.

When Misty walked in she passed by Scrappe and a thick light skinned chick with a messed up weave sitting on the couch. She went directly to Giz, who was sitting on his computer, "What up Cuzz? I missed you." She said as she gave him a kiss on the cheek. He stood up and gave her a hug. "I missed you too Cuzzo. I was beginning to wonder if you were ever coming back. I heard that you were out in Vegas makin enemies." Giz said.

Misty looked over at Scrappe and back to Giz as she said, "You know how these emotional ass niggaz act when I leave 'em. I ain't worried about none of these niggaz." She looked back to Scrappe and his bitch then back at Giz and continued talking, "Fuck them and they knock off ass bitches."

"Bitch do you have a problem?" The bitch sitting next to Scrappe said. "Bitch stay in yo muthafuckin place, which is silent sittin up under dat nigga. Scrappe you couldn't control me but you better control that bitch before she get beat the fuck up." Misty snapped.

Giz grabbed Misty and said, "Chill out Cuzzo." "I'm good Cuzz." Misty said. "Don't trip Giz. This bitch ain't gon say nothing else. She ain't no hard headed tramp." Scrappe said, as he looked at Misty with the devil in his eyes. "I'd rather be a hard headed tramp, than a scary punk bitch any day. But anyways Cuzz, can you take me to the airport in about an hour. I'm going out of town. I just wanted to bring you your car back." Misty said. "Where you going now, Cuzzo?" Giz asked. "I'll tell you later cuzz I don't want mutha fuckas stalking me." Misty said as she walked in the other room. She heard Scrappe let out a cynical laugh.

As she was getting enough money out of her safe for her trip she heard the door close. When she looked up she seen Scrappe standing there with anger in his eyes. "Bitch if you keep on I'm gon continue where I left off in Vegas." He said. "And you'll end up like that nigga on Sunset. Now leave me alone and go take yo bitch to get a better weave." Misty said.

Just then Giz walked in. "Y'all good?" He asked. "We are just fine. I need a blunt and a drink before I get on this plane." Misty said as she walked pass them to get out of the room. She was happy that Giz walked in because she could see in Scrappe's eyes that he was about to trip out, and that would have put Giz in a bad position.

An hour later she was at the airport. Giz was not happy that she was going to Houston, but he figured the same thing that Lil Giz did. Misty was going to do what she wanted to do.

She wasn't exactly sure why she chose to go to Houston. She just knew that Vegas was getting too hectic and that she needed to get away from what was happening between her and Lil Giz.

REUNITED

"Houston, here I come." Misty said to herself as she boarded her first class flight. During the flight she tried to come up with a game plan, but her mind kept drawing blanks. She finally said fuck it and just took a nap.

When she arrived she took a taxi to America's Extended Stay on the 59 just off of Westheimer. The last time she was in Houston she made a lot of money in this area. She was hoping that the money would still flow. Houston was a lot different from Cali and Vegas. Out here there were two options either you work the tracks, which were cheap, but fast, or you worked in one of the "Spas" which were slow but productive. Misty decided to stick with the tracks because she did not have the patience to sit in a "spa" with a bunch of other bitches and wait for money to come. She was a go getter and that is exactly what she intended to do, go get it.

There were three main tracks that Misty felt comfortable working in Houston, but in her reality everywhere she went there was a potential trick, so she stayed ready at all times. She decided to stay close to the room until she put her ears to the streets and and found out what was really going on.

Two days had passed and she had only made $1260. For some hoes this would have been cool, but not for Misty, she was starting to get extremely frustrated. She decided to head across town over to Bissonet. Bissonet was a little on the ghetto side but she knew quite a few people over there, mostly niggaz that wanted her, but they would definitely help out and look out.

She wasn't there long enough to catch a date before she heard "Cali, is that you?" from a car that was in the process of making a u-turn. Cali was what they called her Houston and she didn't mind, so she answered to it. "Hop in." He said as he pulled up on her. She couldn't remember who he was but his face was definitely familiar, so she jumped in. "Yep, it's me, I forgot your name though. It's been a while." She said as she was closing the door. "Q, Shorty G's home boy." As soon as Misty heard the name Shorty G she was instantly put at ease.

Shorty G was a D Boy that she got involved with

last time she was in Houston. He took her from a pimp that she was with and he almost succeeded in taking her out of the game, until he started having baby momma drama, which Misty did not tolerate at all.

"So where is he at?" Misty asked. "We on our way to 'em right now. You don't know how much he need you right now." Q said with a huge smile on his face. Q turned the music up, Z-Ro was blasting, and Misty sat back and enjoyed the ride. When they pulled up Q got on his phone. "A patna, come on outside. I gotta saprise, fo ya Bruh." He hung up.

Shorty G was short exactly like his name implied. He was 5'4" about 170 lbs., a smooth chocolate complexion, and a sexy raspy voice. He wasn't the best in the appearance department but his personality made up for everything. When Misty seen him she instantly got a huge smile on her face, remembering all of the fun times that they had together. When he seen her he lit up like a christmas tree. "Cali, where the hell you been Lil Mama. You gotta make me some stuffed bell peppers!" He said as he wrapped his arms around her, lifted her up and twirled her around. Before she could say anything he kissed her with a passion that told her that he needed, wanted, desired, and yearned for her.

"Okay, Shorty let's take this in the house before our clothes are on the ground in this parking lot." Misty said. Shorty G thanked Q about a thousand times and invited him up for a drink, which he declined because he wanted to leave them alone to catch up. All of Shorty's friends took a likin' to Misty and they all looked out for her as if she was a part of their family.

"So, where you been Ma, and why did you leave without saying bye?" Shorty asked as he handed Misty a drink. "I been around the world and back, and I left because you promised me this great life and just as I was beginning to believe in you, your baby momma started to trip, and I don't deal wit that type of shit." Misty said. "Aww Ma, you should have talked to me about it, and I would have straightened that out." Shorty said. "Yeah, well it is what it is. But look Shorty, I came back out here to get money, not to rekindle our flame. It is nice to have someone familiar and trustworthy to call on, but don't get your hopes up about us. You not gon take me out the game this time." Misty said. "I don't even wanna take you out this time around. You showed me some shit and since you been gone I done had a few hoes, we can get dis money together." Shorty said. "Aww shit, here you go. Nigga you a D Boy, not a Pimp. What happened to your hatred for pimps and you not wantin me to be out there hoeing?" Misty said sarcastically. "Shit, a sign of da times, shit has changed. So you fuckin wit me or not?" Shorty said. "Nigga, you crazy, I can't even respect you as a pimp, and quite honestly I don't fuck wit pimps no more anyways." Misty said. "Just think about it, but for now we got some makin up ta do." Shorty said as he took Misty's drink out of her hand, picked her up, and carried her into his room.

Misty knew what this would lead to, but she remembered how good the dick was and could not resist. He laid her down on the bed and undressed her slowly as he kissed every part of her body. They made love for what seemed like hours. As good as it felt, in the back of her mind all Misty could think about was that she could not get caught up. She came out here on a mission and she was going to stick to it.

When they finally decided to go to sleep he held her as tight as he possibly could, because he had a feeling that if he didn't she was not going to be there when he woke up. And he was right because she was already planning to leave.

As soon as Misty heard him snoring she eased out of bed, put her clothes on and left. She made her way back to Bissonet and got to work. Things were moving fast as she went on date after date, but they were so cheap that it wasn't adding up fast enough for her. After five dates she barely had $400.

Just as she decided to head back to her room Shorty G pulled up on her. "Get'n the car Cali." He said in a tone that said he was trying to be cool. Misty knew that he had somewhat of a temper, and she also didn't want to spend any money on a taxi, so she got in the car. "Why did you leave without telling me?" He asked. "Because I ain't got time to be all lovey dovey, I got money to make Shorty. And you not gon do nothin but distract me like you did last time. Now can you take me back to my room off the 59?" Misty said. Shorty didn't say anything for a minute. He was trying to figure out how to get her back. He was driving towards the room so Misty wasn't tripping. After a few minutes, he said,"look Cali, as long as you out here you ain't got no choice but to fuck wit me." "Nigga, you have lost your mind if you think that you gon make me fuck wit you. You can drop me off and be gone. As a matter of fact you can pull over right here and this can all be done." Misty said. "What room you stayin at? I ain't pulling over nowhere." He said. "America's Extended Stay" Was all Misty said. Shorty turned up the music and neither one of them said another word.

When he pulled up she just got out of the car and headed towards her room. He hurried up and parked a followed behind her. She thought about locking him out but decided not to. So as she cleaned herself up and got dressed for the day she listened to him talk about how much money they could make together and she let it all go in one ear and out the other.

"I hear you Shorty, and I will think about it but as of now can you drop me off on Hilcroft so i can get back to work." Misty said as she was switching purses to one that matched her outfit. Shorty didn't show any signs of being annoyed but inside he was annoyed as hell, because he knew that she wasn't really going to give it any thought.

As soon as he dropped her off before he hit the corner he seen her jumping in another car out of his rearview mirror. At that point he made up his mind that he wasn't going to give up that easily.

Misty stayed down on Hillcroft all evening and

most of the night. When she finally had her last trick

bring her back to her room it was going on 4am. She

was satisfied because she had made a little over $900,

but she was tired as hell. Shorty had given her some

weed so she rolled a blunt and smoked as she soaked in

the tub, until she fell asleep.

FAKE ASS PIMP

It seemed as if only a few minutes had went by when she heard a knock at the door. She looked at the clock and it said 10:27, and the water in the tub was ice cold. "Just a minute." Misty yelled as she got out of the water and wrapped herself in a towel. When she looked out of the peephole she could barely see Shorty's face. She opened the door and said, "I am still tired so if you came to talk then come back later." And she got in the bed and bundled herself in the covers. Shorty got in the bed next to her and just watched her as she laid there sleeping.

When Misty woke up, she smelled bacon. She grabbed a robe and went into the other room. Shorty was in the small makeshift kitchen of the suite cooking. "Oh, so you have learned how to cook since I been gone." MIsty said playfully. "Just a lil bit." He replied. He sat a plate down in front of her and took a seat. They ate a caught up on lost time for a while.

When he finally built up the nerve, he told her that he had a hoe and wanted to take her to Florida, but he didn't really know what to do. Florida was one of the places that Misty hadn't been to yet but wanted to go, so she decided to take him up on his offer.

Two days later, Shorty had rented a car and was ready to go. He picked up Misty first. "Cali, please do not be rude and run her off, she is my only source of income right now." Shorty said. "I am gon be me regardless, and if she don't like it then I don't know what to tell 'er." Misty said with an attitude. When they pulled up Misty seen a light skinned, slightly overweight, but pretty in the face mixed chick walking up to the car. "Workable." she thought to herself. Shorty knew that Cali was not going to get in the back so he said, "You drive." as he hopped out of the car. Misty already knew why he did that so she climbed into the driver seat.

Shorty got in the front and the other chick got in the back. "Tatiana, this is Cali. Cali this is Tatiana." He said. Before Misty could say anything Tatiana started talking, and it seemed like she would never shut up. They were not even 10 minutes into their trip and Misty was thoroughly annoyed.

Fifteen hours later they were riding down Orange Blossom Trail in Orlando Florida. Misty noticed enough hoes to know that there was some money to get but not enough to be excited about. So they found a room about a mile away from the track. "I don't know what y'all are about to do, but I need to get a few hours of sleep before I get down." Misty said. "Bitch y'all gon sleep when I tell you to sleep." Shorty G said, like he was really a pimp. Misty almost tripped out but she knew that he had an impression to hold up with the other bitch. So she shot him a look that could kill and bit her tongue.

Tatiana was oblivious to what was going on. As soon as she got into the shower Misty let his ass have it. "Let me explain something to you. I don't give a fuck about what you have going on with this dumb ass bitch. I am not your bitch and you are not going to treat me like I am. I do what I want, when i want, and how I want. I run my own program. Now you want me to teach this bitch and I agreed to do so but you gon have to figure out how to make her think that you are actually a pimp without pissing me off. Because I will leave you and that bitch out here stranded, without a second thought." Feeling like less of a man because of the way he was just spoke to, Shorty had to say something to redeem himself but not piss her off because he knew that she meant everything that she said. "Look, you are ma bitch, you just not ma hoe. And I need you to teach her how ta be our hoe so you can chill out and be wit me. Now can you please just play this out and let me run things?" Shorty pleaded. "Shorty, please. Watch how you talk to me and I will teach her how to be yo hoe cuzz I don't need nor do I want one. I don't even like bitches, and you know that. Now I am going to go get my own room so I don't have to deal with this dumb ass shit. I will be ready to work in about three hours. I will call you and let you know what room number I am in as soon as I get it." Misty said as she grabbed her bag and was out the door.

About an hour later Shorty was knocking on Misty's door. Annoyed because he woke her up she got up and opened the door. The first thing she saw was a bottle of Remy and a blunt. "Here is my peace offering." Shorty said. Misty laughed and said, "I still ain't yo bitch." They laid on the bed and drank the Remy straight from the bottle and smoked.

After that Misty was ready to get some money.

"Tell yo bitch to be ready in 30 minutes. We gon need to take the car so I can check things out and after this time you can either drop us off or we can take a taxi." Misty said. "Ok Lil Mama, she gon be ready just come knock on her door when you are ready ta go." Shorty said as he walked out the door.

It was about 7pm when they hit the track. Misty drove around and scoped out the different trick rooms, good corners and parking lots to work, and then found a few designated spots for Tatiana to take car dates to. Tatiana was still green, but she knew enough to get some money without her hand being held. So they parked and got to work.

"Look Tot, can I call you Tot?" Not waiting for an answer Misty carried on. Only take tricks to the motels that I showed you or the spots that I showed you, that way I will always know where to find you once we separate. Other than that, be safe and let's get this money.I'm gon cross the street cuzz i work better alone." Misty said. "Can we just stay together until one of us catches a date, I am kind of scared, I have never worked outside of Houston before." Tatiana asked. Misty too a deep breath and said, "Ok, but if one of us don't catch within 20 minutes then we have to split up." They continued walking together.

Tatiana was more interested in telling Misty her life story than she was in getting some money and Misty was not feeling that at all. "Look when we go in then you can come to my room and talk all you want but as of now you need to focus on getting some money, you got a, no, we got a pimp to pay and that is what we need to be focusing on. Now when we get to this next light either you need to cross over or I do." Misty said in a slightly annoyed voice.

Before they got to the light MIsty was hopping in a car. "Thank God", she thought to herself. About 45 minutes later Misty was finished and there were what seemed like 100 police cars on the track. She had the trick drop her off at the car. As she was walking up to it Tatiana appeared from behind a bush. "The police are everywhere I didn't know what to do so I just got a ride back to the car." She said. "Did you get some money?" Misty asked. "No, I didn't catch." Tatiana replied. "Wow, you got a ride, but no money." Misty said irritatingly."You don't ever get in a trick's car and get out wit no money. Don't you know that some tricks get off just by being in a hoes presence. You got a lot to learn, sweetheart." Misty said.

Misty couldn't understand how bitches were so fucking dumb. Nobody ever had to hold her hand and teach her shit. When she turnt out all she needed was a conversation about how to tell if she was dealing with the police and she was good.

So they made it back to the hotel and Tatiana went to her room and Misty went to hers. Misty was not surprised to find Shorty in her room, but she was quite annoyed by it because she knew that she didn't give him a key. "Why you back so soon? It hasn't even been two whole hours?" Shorty asked. "There was entirely too much police activity. But why the hell are you in my room, and how did you get in here? Are much better questions." Misty said with an attitude. "I grabbed your extra key off of the table earlier. How much did y'all make?" Shorty said. "What I made is my business, and you need to talk to your bitch about what she did or didn't make." MIsty said as she began undressing for a shower. "You are ma bitch, and I'm asking what both of y'all made because you supposed to have it all in ya hand ready to give to me before you walk through the door." Shorty said. "You must really think you ma pimp. Shorty you got me fucked up I ain't givin you shit. You need to leave before we really get into it." Misty snapped, as she was getting in the shower.

She wasn't in the shower for 30 seconds before

the curtain flew open and Shorty grabbed her by her hair and drug her to the bed. He climbed on top of her and put his hand around her throat. "Listen to me. You ma bitch, ma hoe, ma slut, and any other thing that I want you to be. I been being nice to you because of the love that I have for you but I see that's not workin. Now I'm gon show you why that other bitch listens so well." Misty was too busy trying to gasp for some air to fight back. With his free hand Shorty undid his belt and proceeded to whip Misty like she was a child. And he never let go of her throat. The last thing Misty remembers was him standing up, his right hand still around her throat, and the belt in his left hand coming down on her stomach. Then she blacked out.

When she woke up she was covered up and

Tatiana was sitting at the foot of the bed. It took her a minute to realize that this was reality and not a dream, but the stinging sensation that she felt all over her body let her know that it was all real.

"Why the fuck are you in ma room, and where da fuck is dat nigga at? Misty snapped as she jumped up and went straight for her stash to make sure all of her money was still there, and putting on a long shirt. She was sure that he took the $175 out of her purse, so she didn't even bother looking for that. "He just came to ma room and gave me a key and told me to come over here and then he left." Tatiana said. "Look, I don't wanna be fucked up towards you but you need to get the fuck out of ma room, i don't even know why he told you to come over here." Misty said. "Well, he told me not to leave your room until he got here, so I can't leave. You should just listen to him because from what I can see he was light on you, it get's a lot worse." Tatiana said as she lifted up her shirt to show Misty all of permanent whelps across her stomach and back. "Bitch, you are stupid as fuck if you gon let any nigga scare and beat you into doing what they want you to do. I ain't that type bitch. So like I said get the fuck outta my room before we have a mutha fuckin problem." Misty said as she was walking to the door to open it for her.

As soon as she open the door she seen Shorty G standing there. "Nigga you got me fucked up. I ain't this dumb ass bitch, now take yo hoe and get the fuck outta ma room. You ain't no muthafuckin pimp anyways, you a D Boy." Misty yelled. "Bitch lower yo muthafukin voice befo' I cave yo fuckin face in. Tatiana go fill the trash can up with ice and get yours outta yo room and fill that one up wit ice too and bring them both here." Shorty said, as he was in Misty's face, never taking his eyes from hers.

Misty was trying to figure out how to get out of this situation, and why the fuck he needed two trash cans full of ice. "Look Shorty, it don't matter what you do to me, the first chance I get I'm outta here, and you lucky I couldn't get on the plane wit ma piece or you would be dead by now." Misty said in a very calm voice. "I see you lowered yo tone, that tells me that you are learning, now if you just learn how to control yo smart ass mouth we will be just fine." Shorty said calmly just before he backhanded Misty in her mouth. "What the fuck do you keep hitting me for Shorty?" Misty asked in a voice filled with anger. "Cuz bitch you gon learn to respect me one way or another, and don't worry. We can stay in this room for as long as it takes. Which shouldn't be long." Shorty said.

There was a knock on the door. Shorty reached and opened it. It was Tatiana with the ice. "You know what to do bitch. After you do it catch a taxi to the track and get back to work. And don't come back to this muthafuckin room wit less than $500 or you know what's gon happen." Shorty said.

Misty was really tripping now. "Did this nigga take gorilla pimpin 101 since the last time she seen him" She thought to herself. "Now bitch, back to you. Like I said, one way or another you gon respect me." He said, and then ripped her shirt off of her.

Most women would have felt exposed by this, but Misty didn't care who seen her naked. She was just pissed by the whole situation and even more pissed that she put herself in it. She figured that there was only two ways for her to get out of this. Either she can start yelling at the top of her lungs and hope that someone called the police before he knocked her out. Or, she would have to play into his game and make him trust her.

Since Misty was 100% against getting the police involved in anything, she had to go with the second option. She really didn't feel like doing that either because she knew he wouldn't believe her if she just flipped the script immediately. So she would have to let him take his so called method of getting her to respect

him a couple more levels before she submitted to him.

"Here we go, let the games begin." She thought to

herself.

GORILLA

"Look Shorty, why don't you just leave and go about your business, and let me go about mines." Misty said. "Wrong answer." Shorty said just before he shot her another backhand to the mouth. Misty took a deep breath and held in her words. Tatiana came out of the bathroom and went out the door, without saying a word. "How do niggaz get these bitches to that point?" Misty thought to herself.

Shorty grabbed her by the hair and pulled her in the bathroom. The tub was filled up about four inches and filled with ice. "Bitch get in the tub so those whelps will go down, before you be walking around here lookin like that other bitch." Shorty said. "Shorty, fuck you I ain't gettin in that shit. You get in dat cold ass shit." Misty snapped. "I see you not gon make this easy." He said, as he closed the bathroom door. He released her hair and pinned her against the door by her throat. And once again he took his belt off and began whipping her with no mercy. This time Misty couldn't hold back her tears, and he let her get enough air to not pass out. "Ok." was all Misty managed to get out. "You ready to listen now?" Shorty asked as he looked in her eyes with his hand still around her throat and belt in the air. Misty nodded, yes. He whacked her two more times. "I don't understand sign language, bitch." "Yes." Misty gasped.

He whacked her three more times. "Yes, what bitch?"
He said as he loosened the grip on her throat a little.
"Yes, Shorty" Misty cried. He gripped her throat even
tighter and began whipping her even harder and more
furiously, for what seemed like forever to Misty." Now, I
am going to ask you this again. Yes, what?" Shorty said.
"Yes, Daddy." Misty said through her crying and gasping
for air.

"Good, now get in the fuckin water. Lay all the
way back and don't get up until i tell you to. Do you
understand?" He said. "Yes, I understand." Misty cried
as she was stepping into the tub. Before her foot
touched the water Shorty slapped her and she slipped
in the tub. "Bitch, stop playing wit me. Yes, what?' He
said "Yes, Daddy. I understand." Misty cried, as she got

herself together and laid in the freezing cold tub.

In her entire time on this earth Misty had never been done like this before. Part of her wanted to really give in to him. But an even bigger part wanted to kill his ass. For about 10 minutes, that seemed like hours to Misty, he made her lay in the tub. The entire time he was talking about how she was going to respect him, and get his money, and be obedient. All she could think about was how long she could stand this before she exploded.

"Get out of the tub. There is a bottle of witch hazel on the bed. Dry off and then rub that where ever you see whelps. As a matter of fact, you have so many just put it all over your body." Shorty said. "Can I turn off the air, it is freezing?" Misty asked "If you would have addressed me correctly I would have said yes, but hell naw, freeze until I say otherwise." Shorty said in a cold voice.

Misty had never even imagined that Shorty had such an evil side to him. So along with being pissed, she was shocked. But she did as he said and put the witch hazel on. "Daddy, can I put some clothes on and smoke a blunt please?" She asked. "You can put on a shirt, and that's it. But no blunt. I want you to be completely sober so that you fully understand that I am not playin wit you." Shorty said. "Yes, Daddy" Misty said as she grabbed a shirt out of her bag.

"Now, get over here and sit on the floor in front of me." He ordered. Misty said nothing, she just did what she was told. He leaned down so that they were face to face, and wrapped her hair around his left hand.

"You are going to learn that I am in charge, and that you

belong to me." He said in a very authoritative voice.

"Ok, Daddy." Misty said submissively.

He stood up and yanked her up by her hair. He

then bent her over the bed and proceeded to violently

penetrate her analy without any lube. Misty let out a

scream when he first entered her. She was no virgin to

anal sex, but her ass was still tight and a big dick with no

lube hurt like hell. "Bitch, the more noise you make the

harder I'm gon fuck you." Shorty said. Misty tried to be

quiet, but she couldn't. So his strokes kept getting

harder and harder.

Misty had this underlying yearning for rough sex.

In the bed she was completely submissive and wanted a

man to take it. The rougher. the better. But in this particular situation she needed to fight the pleasure that she was getting. But when it came down to it her body gave into him.

"Oh, bitch you like this. You like when Daddy punishes dat ass. Yo pussy is drippin all over me." Shorty said. "Yes Daddy, I like it!" Misty yelled out. Shorty fucked her harder and harder. Misty was going crazy over what she was feeling. He flipped her over, put her legs up and plunged into her soaking wet, but still tight pussy. "Damn bitch, I shoulda been fuckin yo ass like this since day one. You definitely ain't goin nowhere now." Shorty said. He grabbed her throat and squeezed tight, then slapped her three times. "Who do you belong to, bitch?" He asked. "I belong to you, Daddy."

MIsty replied. "That's right, now you got it. You gon be a good hoe and go get ma money?" He asked as he took a long deep stroke. "Yes, Daddy, I'm gon get yo money like a good hoe." She squealed. 'I don't believe you bitch, I think you need yo ass whooped a few mo times." He said and then pulled out and put her back in the doggystyle position. "Daddy, no, please. I don't need to be whipped anymore. I promise." Misty said as she seen him reaching for his belt. "Bitch shut up and take what you got coming." He said as he shoved his dick in her ass as hard as he could. Misty let out another scream. "Does it hurt, hoe?" He asked. "Yes, Daddy. It hurts." Misty cried.

"How, about this hoe? Does this hurt?" Shorty said and gave her a deep hard stroke and a whack across her back. Misty screamed. He kept on giving her long hard strokes and whacks on the back until he exploded inside of her. She was crying from pain, pleasure, and anger as she collapsed on the bed and passed out.

She woke up to him gently putting witch hazel on her back. She let out a few sighs of pain. "It's ok Baby. Daddy is gon take care of you. You just have to learn how to listen and respect me." Shorty said in that loving voice that Misty knew. "I know Daddy, I am just not used to being controlled anymore, but I understand, I promise. And I am going to do better." Misty said submissively. He grabbed the back of her neck and pushed her head into the pillow. "Please don't bring that side out of me again, it will only get worse. Do you understand?" He said in a stern but still quite loving voice.

Misty thought to herself that nigga is certifiably crazy. And she could not figure out how or why she let herself get put in this position. "Yes, Daddy." She replied. "Can I please smoke a blunt, because I am in so much pain right now. My entire body is sore," Misty asked. "Yeah, Mama, you can smoke. Tatiana will be over here in about 30 minutes or so and y'all gon smoke together while I go check out these streets." He said. "I really don't feel like being around her. Can I smoke by myself, please?" Misty said. "There you go thinking you are running things again. Now like I said, Tatiana is coming over here to smoke with you while I go check out these streets. Now, do you understand or do I have to make you understand?" Shorty said sternly. "I understand, Daddy." Misty replied. "That's better. Now turn over so Daddy can show you how good bitches get treated." Shorty said.

Misty did as she was told and turned over. Her back was on fire, but she didn't complain. Shorty opened her legs and gave her some of the best head that she has ever gotten. She had forgotten how gifted he was with his tongue. Just as she was about to cum there was a knock on the door. "Don't move." Shorty said as he went to the door. He came right back and continued where he left of. "Cum for Daddy, bitch. Let me know that you appreciate me." He said. "Yes, Daddy. I'm almost there."Misty moaned. About two minutes later Misty came so hard that she went into convulsions. Shorty couldn't help but to fuck her after she came that hard. He climbed on top of her and slid his big dick into her already throbbing pussy. "Damn, Ma. Why is yo pussy so fuckin good?" He said as he stroked her slow and gentle, but still deep. With every stroke Misty felt her pussy gripping onto him tighter and tighter. He felt it too. "Daaaaddy, Daaaaaaaaddy, I'm gon cum again." Misty managed to get out. "No, Ma. Not yet. Hold it in fo Daddy. You hear me. Show me that you can listen. Don't cum until I tell you to." He said. "Yeeees, Daaaaddy. I'm holding it in." Misty said. But she didn't know how much longer she could hold back. His dick felt so good stroking her pussy. He started going faster and harder. "Pleeeeeaaasssse, Daaaaaddy, let me cuuuuuum." She screamed. "Go ahead, bitch cum wit

Daddy.Cum right now, bitch!" He said. Misty let go. Her pussy started pulsating on his dick, her entire body tensed up, and she couldn't breath. He hit it even harder and faster and let out a loud sound and gave her one last hard thrust and the came together.

He got up, wiped his dick off, and straightened his clothes. And before he opened the door he licked Misty's pussy a few more times then put the cover over her. When he opened the door Tatiana was standing right there. He pulled her in and turned around so that he could see Misty and gave Tatiana a long wet tongue kiss, the whole time never taking his eyes off of Misty.

Misty thought to herself, this nigga is trifling. She knew that Tatiana could taste her pussy. And that bitch didn't even say anything about it. It ain't no way in hell....Misty thought then she thought fuck it, not her problem. "Y'all smoke, get cha minds right and then get ready for work. I will be back in about two hours to get y'all." Shorty said as he was walking out the door.

HOUSTON NIGGAZ

Shorty was feeling pretty confident about teaching Misty a lesson, and winning her over with "his love". So he went out to the track and chopped it up with a few other pimps and had a drink.

Misty was trying her hardest not to call Tatiana all kind of stupid, retarted bitches. She just tuned her out and smoked and got prepared for the night. She couldn't make the calls that she needed to make because she was sure that Tatiana was instructed to tell everything. So Misty just played along and acted like she learned her lesson.

Before they left out to go get in the car with Shorty Misty went in the bathroom and put her stash in a condom and stuffed it. She knew that he wouldn't

check her before they went out. As soon as he dropped

them off Misty jumped in the first car that pulled over.

She was very pleased that this particular trick was very

easy going and not in a rush. He wanted a quickie for

180 and he was willing to get the room.

So after he came, Misty asked him could he drop

her off at the airport. He could sense that she was in

some kind of trouble and he had seen the fresh whelps

on her back while they were doing it doggy style. So he

agreed without asking any questions. When they arrived

to the airport he gave her his number and told her to

call him if she found herself in another bind. Misty

thanked him and got out of the car.

As soon as she got out of the car she called Y.T,

because she knew that he had the hook up on plane tickets. "What bitch?" Y.T. answered. "My nigga can you book me a flight from Orlando, to Houston and I will send you the money as soon as I touch down." Misty asked "What da fuck you don got cha self in now?" Y.T. asked. Misty could tell that he was in one of his fuck you moods. "I just got stranded. I didn't bring enough money wit me and it's all bad out here right now." Misty explained. "Bitch, who you tryna run game on, I just talked to ma patna out dere and he eatin. So whateva sucka ass nigga you went out dere wit you need ta get back wit." Y.T. said "Fuck you, Y.T." Misty said and hung up.

Misty went ahead and paid full price for her ticket and got back to Houston. She knew she couldn't stay at the same hotel because within a day or two Shorty would be at her door. So she moved to the Red Roof Inn off of Hilcroft. It was a lot less than she desired, but it would do. She wouldn't be there long.

A couple days went by, and except for the phone calls that she expected, there was no sign of Shorty. Until she she jumped out of a car and seen Shorty hitting the corner. "Shit" she thought to herself. "Get in da car Cali." Shorty yelled out. Misty treated him like any other pimp and did an about face and walked the opposite way. This went on for about 30 minutes before she was able to get back to her room unseen. So she thought.

About 20 minutes after she was in her room she heard a bang at the door. She didn't say anything. He kept banging. "I know you in dere Misty. Open da fuckin

doe!" He yelled. "How the fuck did he know what room

I was in." Misty said to herself. "I'm gon sock this fuckin

maid in her jaw if one of y'all don't open this mutha

fuckin doe, Misty!" "I don't give a fuck Shorty, that's

between you and that maid. I ain't openin shit." Misty

yelled back. This went on for about two minutes. Misty

didn't want the hotel to all the police and kick her out

so she decided to open the door. After Misty had her

money safely hidden she opened the door.

She was expecting him to trip out and put his

hands on her. This nigga walked in, laid on the bed

closest to the door, and said, "Gimme a massage, Cali."

Misty looked at him like he was stupid. "I ain't givin you

no fuckin massage Shorty. What the fuck do you want? I

don't wanna fuck wit yo crazy ass so you are wastin your time." Misty said as she sat on the other bed. "Just Gimme a massage Cali." Was all he said.

Misty's phone rang, and she silenced it. "Who da fuck is callin you, dat you can't answer in front of me?" Shorty said. "Why da fuck you worried about who callin me? Who be callin you?" Misty said as she grabbed his phone. He didn't even budge when she grabbed it.

She pretended to be looking for female names, saying every female's name that she seen, out loud. But really she was looking for his best friend Jono's number, because she knew that he was one of the only people that Shorty ever listened to. As soon as she seen his number she picked up the hotel phone and called him.

"Hey Jono, this is Cali. How have you been?" Misty said when she heard him pick up. "Hey, Cali, what's been up, I heard you was back in town. Shorty been hidin you." He said. "He ain't been hidin me, I been hidin from him. This nigga is crazy. Can you please tell him to leave out of my room, cuzz I don't wanna fuck wit him no more." Misty said. "I'mma tell you like this Cali, as long as you in Houston it ain't but two niggaz you can fuck wit and that's Shorty or me. Cuz Shorty ain't gon go fo seeing you wit anotha nigga unless it's me." Jono said. "Y'all niggaz are both crazy. I ain't gotta be wit nobody. Can you just tell him to leave ma room and give me time to think and if I decide to stay in Houston then I will fuck wit him and other than that I will leave." Misty pleaded. "Aiight. put 'em on da phone." Jono said. "Thank you." Misty said as she handed the phone to Shorty. Shorty listened for a minute then said. "Aiight bruh. Already." Then handed her the phone back. "He ain't gon trip out, he gon leave in a minute. He just wanna talk to ya." Jono said. "Ok, thank you, Jono." Misty said and then hung the phone up.

Misty was relieved after talking to Jono. Her and Shorty went back and forth about being together for about an hour, before he just gave up and left. Misty was happy that he finally decided to leave, because she was quite irritated.

A couple of days later she got a call from him. She wasn't going to answer it, but something told her to. "Hey Shorty, what's up?" she asked. "Look Cali I ain't tryna bother you. I'm on my way to the airport. You was my last hope of stayin out here, cuz I can't do what I know anymore. I'm sorry I did you how I did, I just thought that was how a pimp was supposed to act. In reality all I ever wanted to do was be your man and take you away from all that. I understand and respect your decision. My rent is paid for the next two months. Jono has the key, you can stay there if you want, I know you hate stayin in rooms. And again, ma bad for doing what I did." Then he hung up.

Misty didn't really know how to feel. She felt bad but she also felt like he did that shit to himself. And she couldn't understand why he got his hopes up over her when she never told him that she would stay and be with him. Fuck it she thought, and she carried on working.

At the end of the night she called Jono and asked him could he come get her and take her back to Shorty's. He was there to pick her up within 20 minutes. He was the same old cool ass Jono as she remembered. He took her back to his spot because there was no power at Shorty's spot anymore. She wasn't trippin, she knew she was safe so she went along. When they got to his spot they chopped it up for a while then he gave her some covers and a pillow and told her that the couch was hers.

When she woke up the next morning Jono and his girl were sitting at the table eating breakfast. "I made you a plate. It's in the microwave." Jono's girl said. "Thank you, I am starving. I don't even remember the last time I ate."Misty said as she got up and started folding her covers. Misty was always extra neat when she was in someone else's house.

"Cali, this is my girl Lil Bit, Lil that's Cali." Jono said "Nice to meet you, thank you for letting me crash here last night, I will get the power on today so I can get outta y'all space." Misty said. "I'm not trippin, Jono told me all about you. I don't mind helpin out. Anybody that he has love for has ma love too." Lil Bit replied. "That's what's up. Do you mind if I use you your bathroom before I eat?" Misty asked. Lil Bit showed Misty to the bathroom up stairs.

Lil Bit was was about 5', maybe 110lbs., she had a pretty dark complexion, and for a small girl she had curves. Misty was in the bathroom for about 30 minutes. When she came out she was dressed and ready to start her day.

"So where did Shorty go?" Misty asked Jono as she was heating up her plate. "He got a baby momma in New York so he decided to go up there wit her." Jono said. "Oh ok. Why did he have to leave from here?" Misty asked. "He can't catch no mo dope cases out here. Da laws is on 'em. That's why he was so happy to see you. He thought y'all could make somethin' happen cuz he know you a go getta." Jono said. "I understand, but I didn't come out here ta save him. I came out here to get money. And even if I wanted to be wit him that nigga showed me a side of him that turned me all the way off." Misty said. "I know ma boy get crazy sometimes but he got alotta love fo you Cali. And I'm gon be honest. When you called me and put him back on da phone, I told him that he bet not leave that room wit out you or he stupid as hell." Jono said. Misty laughed, "Y'all niggaz is crazy." "You good fo Shorty, Cali. I knew dat the first time round. We was all mad when you disappeared, but I knew why." Jono said. "Yeah, well what is meant to be will be. When do you think you can take me to get the power turned on so I can be outta yo way?" Misty asked. "Gimme, about an hour and we can go do dat." Jono said as he headed up stairs.

While Misty was waiting for Jono to get ready she decided to check in with Giz and Lil Giz. They were both a little worried, but all was well. Misty was kind of ready to go back to Vegas. The whole ordeal with Shorty had pretty much drained her. And she was not sure if

moving into his apartment was such a great idea. She

decided to think that through some more.

When Jono came down the stairs he said, "I'm

ready, let's roll." "You know what Jono, I don't even

know if it is such a great idea for me to stay in his

apartment after what me and him just went through.

Would it be ok if I stayed here for a few days while I

figure out ma next move?" Misty asked. "You know it's

whatever wit me Cali, you are always welcomed, but let

me talk to Lil Bit about it." Jono replied. "Ok, cool. For

right now I am just gon take off on foot and see what I

can get out here. I will be back in a few hours. Will you

have talked to her by then?" Misty said. "Already Ma, I'll

let you know when you get back. You be safe and call

me if you need me." Jono said.

Jono was about 5'10", 170 lbs., bright skinned, and had a real laid back demeanor. He was one of those people that nobody really had anything bad to say about. He was solid. He was a few years older than Shorty and he looked out for him like he was his nephew. From the first day him and Misty met he looked out for her just as he did for Shorty, and she respected him just as Shorty did.

HOUSTON BREEDS D BOYS

A few days turned into a couple of weeks. Everything was going ok. Lil Bit and Misty were getting along great. Lil Bit was a go getta as well. She worked the strip clubs, and she was good at it. She encouraged Misty to try it out. But that didn't go too well.

As beautiful as Misty was she just couldn't manage to make good money in the strip club environment. For one she was not a dancer, and even if she was she had a mental block that did not allow her to get all sweaty and worked up for dollar bills.

So three days into this strip club adventure the manager at the club told Misty that she had enough time to warm up and she had to take the stage. Misty was not feeling that at all. So she pulled Lil Bit into the dressing room. "Girl he wants me to get on stage, and I do not know how to dance." Misty exclaimed. "Don't trip, just pop a pill and you will be fine." Lil Bit said. "Shit, I been poppin pills that shit ain't gon work, I don't even like being high while I'm trying to get some money. Don't trip though I will figure something out." Misty said. "Aiight, Ma. Let me get back out here to dis money." Lil Bit said as she was walking out of the dressing room.

Misty went back out on the floor and tended to this trick named Mike. He wasn't her typical trick, then again no one in the club was her typical trick. They were all hood niggaz, but this particular one Misty knew that he had some real money, and she kind of took a little liking to him and he took a huge liking to her. "What's up Baby, You tryna get outta here and go do somethin?"

Misty whispered in his ear. "Fa sho, I'm ready when you are." He excitedly replied.

"So what made you wanna leave with me tonight, Lil Mama?" Mike asked as they were pulling out of the parking lot. "Because you seem like the kind of man that I need right now." Misty replied. "And what kinda man is that?" He asked. "The kind that doesn't mind paying for the best night of his life. Am I right?" Misty said. "Already, Ma. So where we going?" Mike said. "Wherever you gon feel comfortable getting the absolute best head, and most amazing pussy that you have ever had in your life." Misty replied. "Shit, we can go back to ma spot." He exclaimed. "That sounds like a plan to me, but you know that I need to know what you gon do for me." Misty said, trying not to treat him like the typical trick but making sure that it is going to be worth it for her. Mike pulled out a wad of money wrapped in a rubberband and tossed it over to Misty. "Is that cool Lil Mama? And I will take you home in the morning when we wake up." Mike asked "It depends how much it is." Misty said as she was taking the rubber band off and counting the money. "It's a G Ma. But on da cool you gotta be all that I hope you gon be, cuz I don't just be payin fo pussy, I just had ta have yo fly, sexy ass." Mike said.

Satisfied after she counted the money, not really caring what the fuck he was talking about Misty said, "Don't trip Daddy, I can tell you don't be on this shit like that. I be seeing you in the club takin care of yo business. That's why I chose you. Now drive faster so I can hurry up and feel that big dick for real and not through yo pants during a lap dance." Misty said seductively.

Houston was different from most other places that Misty worked. In Houston niggaz were some of her best clients. But they had to be handled differently than her typical trick. They knew they had to pay, and the ones that had it didn't mind paying well, but they needed to feel like they were the man. And Misty had no problem with that at all, especially since damn there all of them had pipe and knew how to slang it.

The part where things got difficult for Misty is that she was a sucker for a nigga with some good dick, especially when he had his shit together. That is how she got caught up with Shorty, although Shorty made it clear that he was not a trick from the beginning, he made himself available in other ways that she needed. But Mike, he was different. He was a trick, but he was also a D Boy that was doing very well for himself. And it did not hurt that he was fine as hell.

He was 6'2", about 220, milk chocolate smooth skin, a baby face, clean cut, taper fade with waves for days, and tastefully tatted up. He dressed down in jeans and t shirts. At least that is what an untrained eye would think, but MIsty knew differently when she first seen him walking into the restroom, the first night she worked in the club. He was wearing a pair of PRPS Noir jeans, a Moncler t shirt, and Ferragamo sneakers. She was on him from that point on, but she tried not to make it noticeable that she knew he had money like that.

The first night that she seen him, which was only three nights prior, she did not approach him, and she acted as if she didn't notice him, but made sure that he noticed her. And made sure that he knew that she was not the usual thirsty, low budget stripper that he was used to seeing. Like him her attire was far from cheap. She wore a pair of jimmy Choo, black stiletto heels, a black and purple teddy from Frederick's, and she smelled of Annick Goutal, which was a citrus smell that got a lot of attention. And she did just what she wanted, he had his eyes on her all evening, until she disappeared. He had no choice but to come back to see her.

The second night, he sent her a drink and she

brought it over to him and said, "If you want my attention a drink is not the way to get it, and definitely not a fruity drink. I drink Remy sweetheart, straight." She set the drink on his table, shot him a wink, and seductively walked away in a way that said follow me now or lose me forever. He was intrigued, but not quite sold. So he requested a private dance in the back room from her.

"If you are expecting me to take my clothes off for that bullshit $25 like the rest of these chicks then you have me sadly mistaken. If you expect me to shake ma ass, then you are sadly mistaken. And if you think you gon give me $50 to fuck me then you are extremely mistaken. So before you waste your time and money you might wanna get one of these other chicks to take you to the back." MIsty said in her feisty voice. "Calm down LIl Mama, slow ya roll. If I thought you was like the rest this wouldn't even be goin down. Now go tell da DJ Mike said put on "How To Love" Cuz that's my dedication to you. And get cha lil fine ass in da back when it come on. I'll be waitin. Already." Mike said and then walked toward the back.

When Misty walked into the private room in the back Mike was sitting there waiting. "Have a seat Ma I just wanna talk to ya fo a minute." He said as he handed her a double shot of Remy. "and by the way those are unlimited to you whenever you work" He said. "Thank you Baby, and the name is Misty, not Lil Mama." Misty said as she took a seat. "No problem, and I like Lil Mama so that is what I'm callin you. So what's ya story Lil

Mama? Why you in here? I can tell dis ain't you. You betta den dis." He said. "My story is irrelevant at this time. I am here and that is all that matters. ...." They spoke for the duration of the song, he slid Misty $100 and walked out.

Now, she was sitting on his California King bed, in his glamorous yet tastefully decorated room, in his four bedroom home, in Sugar Land. "Make yourself at home Lil Mama, don't get shy on me now. You supposed ta be makin dis da best night of ma life." Mike said as he walked in with a fifth of Remy and two glasses. "You must have read my mind because I was sure gon ask you if you had some Remy. Good job. " Misty said with a smile. "Already, Lil Mama. I got whatever you want. You ain't gotta worry 'bout shit as long as you wit me. So, when you gon let me know what it is you was doin in dat club?" Mike said as he was taking off his shirt and revealed a body that damn there made Misty choke on her drink. "I take it you like what you see. But I'm still waitin to find out who it is that I have in ma bed and how she got here." He said.

"Look you are one fine ass nigga, and maybe in different circumstances I would feel the need to let you know ma background. But now is not the time. You paid me ta do something, and that is what I am gon do. Now come closer so I can undress the rest of you and give you the best night of your life like I promised." Misty said as she sat her drink on the nightstand. Mike let out a slight giggle and opened the top drawer on the chest of drawers that he was standing next to. He pulled out four more wads of money wrapped in rubber bands just like the one he tossed at Misty in the car, and tossed those at her, too. "Lil Mama, do you really think I paid you to come fuck me. I ain't that nigga. I gave you that ta ease yo mind. I don't even wanna fuck. Well' I do, cuz you sexy as fuck, but not like that Ma. Put those in ya purse and relax fo me Mama. Talk to yo boy and let me know who you are. I wanna know you, not da stripper, not da hoe, you." Mike said and then sat on the bed next to Misty.

Misty downed her drink, poured another one, then said, "Mike there is more to me than most people can understand or care to know. I see that you da man and dats cool. But I am not that bitch that is lookin to be saved. I am far from one of those broke charity case bitches that your money impresses. Am I gon take it? Hell yeah, because I am about ma money and I ain't turnin shit down. But don't think for one minute that it impresses me." Misty said with attitude. "Ok, Lil Mama. I hear you. Where you from? Cuz you damn sho not from here." Mike said as he sipped his drink.

They drank and talked about life for a while and around 6am Mike asked where she wanted to be dropped off at. Misty was kind of surprised that he really didn't want to fuck but she was cool with it. As they sat in front of Jono's they spoke a little further. "So will I see you at the club tonight?" MIke asked. "Probably not. As a matter of fact you probably won't see me at all because I think I am going back home today." Misty said. "You gon tell me where home is?"

He asked. "I guess I can. Home is in Cali, but I live in Vegas. I'm not sure which one I am going back to yet but I will figure that out after I make some calls." Misty replied. "Well, I'll tell you what Lil Mama. This how much I wanna get to know you. Gimme a few hours to make some arrangements and I will go with you. You know, just to make sure you get there safely." Mike said. "I am grown, I don't need you to make sure I get anywhere safely. And how do you know I want you to come home with me?" Misty said. "Oh, so you can come home wit me but I can't go home wit you." Mike said. "I don't bring niggaz I don't know home wit me. Just cuz you do dat type of shit don't mean I am. But what you can do is give me your number and I will stay in touch." Misty said. "Already, Lil Mama. I like ya style and I definitely wanna do more than just stay in touch, but I will settle for dat fo now, but not fo long." He said. "You wanna take me to the airport then?" MIsty asked. "Fo sho. What time?" He asked. "Shit, I can be ready to go in ten minutes. I just need to go in grab ma stuff and tell ma peeps I'm out." Misty said. "Ok fo sho. When you go in there tell Jono I said what's up." MIke said and shot Misty a wink.

Misty didn't know what to think at this point but she didn't even bother making a scene about it. She had enough trust in Jono to know that he would not set her up for nothing that would harm her so she let it go. "I sure will. Like I said gimme ten minutes and I will be right back out.

ALL OF THESE NIGGAZ ARE

RETARDED

Misty kind of wanted to stay a little longer and see what Mike was really about, after all he just gave her 5K just to spend not even a complete night with her and he didn't even want to have sex. She was not used to niggaz that really wanted to know about her as a person and she didn't really know how to handle it, but she was intrigued by it.

"Hey Lil Bit, sorry I left last night, but that shit was not for me." Misty said when Lil Bit opened the door. "It's cool girl, I seen when you left and Jono and Mike are pretty good friends so I knew that you were in good hands. That nigga got dough, too. And I have never seen him interested in anybody up dere. He occasionally gets a lap dance, always tips $100, and rarely talks unless he doing business. So you must be sumtin special. You betta fuck wit him girl." Lil Bit said excitedly.

It all sounded good to Misty, and if she was one of those broke desperate bitches then she would be impressed, but something inside of her was not letting her sell what Mike was trying to buy. He could have bought all of the pussy, ass, and head that he wanted, but she was not for sell. He had to come with way more than money to get this one.

"Girl I know he has money, and I know that he wants me, but I have my own money and niggaz out here be tryna tie a bitch down and I ain't got time that. If that's the case Shorty would still be here and we wouldn't be having this conversation right now. I am about to take ma ass back home before I fuck around and be knocked up and sat down out here. I just came to get my stuff and tell you and Jono thank you for the southern hospitality. Mike is about to bring me to the airport right now. He is outside waiting." Misty said as she was heading towards her bag. "I hear you girl, but damn. You are really passing up a good one. Anyways, Jono is still sleep and I ain't wakin dat man up. He be trippin when he get woke up." Lil bit replied.

"Oh my gosh." Misty thought to herself. She hated when broads acted like they was scared to do something simple. "Do you mind if I go wake him up and tell em bye. I don't wanna leave without saying bye for a second time because Jono has always been good to me and I owe him that?" Misty asked, out of respect. "Go 'head. I'm gon stay down here, cause i don't want no parts a wakin him up." Lil Bit said as if she was really scared to wake him up.

"Jono." Misty whispered as she lightly tapped him on his shoulder. Jono was sleeping on his back, so when he opened his eyes the first thing that he seen was Misty. "Hey, Ma what's good. I see you made it home." Jono said with a smile on his face. "Yes, I made it home and by the looks of that smile, you must think your hook up worked." MIsty said with playful attitude. "I know it worked, you went home wit 'em." Jono said as he wiped his eyes and reached for his cigarettes and lighter. "Yeah it worked for me. It actually worked out great for me, but not the way that you think it worked.

Anyways I just wanted to come tell you that I appreciate

you and you will forever and always have my love, but I

need to get back home before one of y'all sexy ass

Houston Niggaz get ahold a me again. Mike is about to

bring me to the airport, he is outside waitin right now.

And by the way he said to tell you what's up." Misty

said. "Already. But is ere'thing cool, you straight. It

wasn't no problems, right?" Jono asked, with concern in

his voice. "Naw everything is fine, I just feel like I need

to get ma ass back home. And I couldn't leave without

saying bye again, and I also wanted to give you this

before I left, too." Misty said as she handed him one of

the money rolls that Mike gave her. "Already, Ma, you

know I'm gon always look out fo ya. Step out so I can

throw sumtin on and walk you out and say what's up to

ma boy." Jono said.

"What's up boy, what's good?" Jono said as he approached Mike's car. "Shit, jus' tryna figure out a way to get Lil Mama ta gimme me a chance." Mike said as he was hoppin out of the car to talk to Jono. "Already, baby. If you take her to da airport and let 'er go you just as much a fool as Shorty mane. If I thought her and Lil Bit would go fo it I woulda handcuffed this one mane. She a go getta fo real." Jono said as he watched Misty get in the car. "Yeah, mane she right, but shit if she wanna go den I ain't gon stop 'er, but I put some shit on 'er brain she'll be back fo me and if not den her loss mane cause I ain't like da rest of dese niggaz out chere." Mike said. "Already, mane. But let me get back in dis house. Hit me later i got some biz to holla at cha 'bout.

Aight Cali, be safe Ma and call me and let me know you made it." Jono said as he was walking away.

MIsty was thinking that it might be nice to spend a few days with Mike just to really see what he is about. He might be someone that could definitely be beneficial to her in more ways than one. "Aight, Lil Mama. Let's get you ta where it is you wanna be. You goin' ta Hobby or Bush?" Mike asked as he started the car. "I don't know just yet. I was thinkin that maybe I could chill wit you for a couple days. Just so we could get to know each other a lil better before I go." Misty said, putting an emphasis on maybe. "And what brought this maybe about....You know what, it don't even matter. You opened da doe now you gon walk through it." Mike said as he turned the music up and pulled out.

Misty immediately turned the music back down and said, "Hold up nigga, I said maybe, that ain't opening the door its barely unlockin' it, slow yo roll." "If I was able to slow ma roll, Lil Mama, I wouldn't do it. And barely unlockin is good enough fo me. Now chill, I gotcha, I promise you in good hands. And when, if you decide ta go I'm gon put you on first class wherever it is you goin' from here." Mike said calmly, but firm enough for MIsty to know that it didn't matter what she said he was not about to drive to the airport, today.

But that did not stop her from speaking her mind. "And what makes you think that I can't get my own first class ticket?" Misty asked with attitude. Mike smiled at her, "Calm down, Lil Mama, stop wit da attitude. I know you can get yo own ticket or yo own whatever fo dat matter. I'm just tryna let you know that I'm gon take care a you. As a matter fact let's go eat and go to da Galleria so I can get you sumtin sexy ta wear fo me." Mike said as he reached over and caressed Misty's thigh. "Ok, I'm calm. Can you answer a question for me? Why is it that you think what you can do for me impresses me?" Misty asked calmly, but still with a hint of attitude. "Now that you have calmed down, work on dat attitude. And I am not tryna impress you wit what I can do fo you. I'm tryna show yo ass how you supposed ta be treated. I see dat you keep yaself in the finest, so why would I give you anything less. Now chill out, enjoy da ride and let me control dese next few days, Lil Mama." Mike said sternly as he turned the music up.

He was almost reminding Misty of polished pimp

the way that he took control of the situation so smoothly. Or at least the way that he thought he took control of the situation. No one really ever controlled Misty, they just took things as far as she let them take it. Maybe all of these tactics worked with other chicks but Misty seen through it all. Now she wanted to know exactly what is was that Mike was into, because she knew damn well that he was not living in that nice ass house, and driving a brand new Audi R8 by selling blow in a strip club. Whatever it was, she had two days to figure it out because she was not about to stay any longer no matter how much he tried to "show her how she should be treated".

After eating breakfast at the French Riviera, a cafe near the Galleria, they went shopping. Despite

Misty not being impressed, she had to admit to herself that it did feel good to go shopping on someone else's dime instead of her own. So, about 5K later Misty had four outfits, two purses, two pair of heels, and her nails were freshly done. And she found it quite sexy that Mike got a manicure while she got her nails filled, she loved a man with nice hands.

"Aight, Lil Mama, I'm gon drop you off at ma spot and go make a few fades. Make yaself at home. Da whole house is open to you, especially da kitchen. All I ask is dat you be fresh and sexy when I get back. Gimme bout 2 hours and den you got me all to yaself fo da night. Is dat a bet?" Mike said as they were pulling in front of his house. "Yeah, dats a bet. And thank you for today. It was refreshing." Misty said as she was opening the door to get out. Mike reached out and grabbed her arm, "Close the door, I wasn't done talking yet." Misty did as she was told and closed the door, "I'm listening." He gently grabbed her chin and gave her slight kiss on her lips, "You gon thank me tonight, Lil Mama. You undastand?" Mike said in a very low, and extremely sexy voice. "Yes, Mike. I understand." Misty said faintly. "Naw, Lil Mama, don't call me Mike. Call me Daddy fa now on." He said as his eyes locked onto hers. Misty took a deep breath, "Hold up, hold up, hold up. Are you a pimp?" MIsty asked with attitude back in her voice. "I thought we took care of that attitude situation. And if I was a pimp would it matter, have I broke you, asked you ta hoe, or treated you like anything other than the high class lady that you are?" Mike said. "Nigga I am not stupid, you cannot talk circles around me. As a matter of

fact, it don't even matter!" Misty said as she opened the

car door, got out and started to walk down the street.

No quicker than she stepped foot on the sidewalk Mike

had the car in park and was directly in front of her.

"Don't make no scene in front ma house and

that is the only warning that you get. Na turn round and

walk to da doe. I'm not gon put ma hands yo. I'm not

gon touch you at all, but I got way too much ta lose and

I ain't gon jeopardize it ova you or nobody else. Don't

play wit me out chere." He said in a very calm and low

voice. Misty knew for a fact that he had work in his

house and she understood very clearly he was not

playing, so she chose not to play with him. She walked

to the door like he said. She waited as he grabbed her

luggage and her shopping bags out of the car.

"Thank you for getting my luggage. You can keep those shopping bags. I am calling a taxi to come get me right now. I should have taken ma ass home this morning when I had the chance." Misty said as she was searching for a taxi's number in her phone. "Put the phone down, before I take it." Mike said as he was opening the door. "Nigga please, I pay fo ma phone, you got me fucked up." Misty snapped.

As they walked in the door he dropped the bags and luggage, snatched the phone out of Misty's hand, and then closed the door and locked it. "I tried to be cool wit yo ass, but I see that don't work so this what it is. You had the chance to leave wit da dough I gave you and you chose to stay. The minute you decided that was the minute you lost control. I ain't bout to play dese games wit you. Look around Lil Mama, do it look like I play games. And naw I ain't no pimp, but I can be. Is dat what you want, you wanna be pimped? Yeah dat's what you want, so tonight you going back to da club and you gon get pimped, and I'm not askin, I'm tellin. Now, go upstairs and get fresh n sexy den come down here n continue thankin me." Mike said in a very calm voice that made Misty nervous. "All y'all niggaz out here need to be certified. If you think I'm bout to do anything you just said you are fuckin stupid, you must don't know shit about me. I don't do shit unless I wanna do it and no I don't wanna be pimped, if I did I have many to choose from that don't got mental disorders..........." Misty was saying until she seen him reach over and pull 9 millimeter out of the top drawer of a table sitting next to his front door.

"Nigga, if you gon shoot me then……." He slapped her on the side of her head with it and said, "I ain't gon shoot cha Lil Mama, but I am gon shut yo ass up. I already told yo ass I ain't bout to play dese games. Now do what da fuck I said before I get upset." Mike said, still in a very calm voice. "You just hit me in ma fuckin head wit a gun. And you not upset?" Misty said as she was rubbing her head. "I tapped you, if would've hit you wouldn't be standin, all you gon have is a bump. And if I was upset I would've used it like it was meant to be used. Now, I ain't gon tell you again. Go upstairs, and get fresh and sexy and come back down." He said as he pointed to the stairs with the gun.

Misty grabbed her luggage and went upstairs. She was trying to figure out how to get the fuck out of there. When she got up to his room she immediately checked the windows. "Good, no bars." she said to herself. She had to move quickly. She grabbed her basketball shorts, a wife beater, tennis shoes, and all of her money out of her bag. She quickly put everything except her shoes on, and stuffed $10,000 in three separate condoms and stuffed them in her pussy. Then she put the remaining $1,700 in her shoes, tied them tight, and grabbed her I.D. and social out of her wallet and put them in her bra.

At this moment she was extremely happy that she was really a tomboy. She jumped out of the window into his huge backyard, that had three big trees. She hopped the gate into the neighbor's yard that was to the left of him, then hopped their gate into the yard of the house behind them. It was a little after 3pm so she was hoping that most people were still at work and no one called the police on her. She went through their yard and came out into the neighborhood directly next to his.

About 7 minutes had gone by since he sent her upstairs, so she figured she had at least another 20 minutes, probably longer, before he realized that she was gone. She had no phone, the nearest main street was about a mile and a half away, and she did not know her way through this neighborhood. "Fuck! What the fuck am I gon do now. I don't know nobody's number by heart except for my dad's, Giz, and PB, and I don't wanna call any of them anyways." She thought to herself.

She seen a lady walking her dog across the street, so she crossed over. "Excuse me, I got turned around jogging which direction is the nearest main street?" Misty asked in her sweet, preppie voice. " Oh if you go up to the stop sign make a right then go down about 2 blocks, until you can't go any more, make a left, then make a right you will come out on Brand Ln." The lady said with a smile. "And that is exactly where I need to be. I am out here visiting and went out for a jog and got lost and turned around. Thank you so much.

Misty was glad that the lady was going in the opposite direction. She pretended to bend down and tie her shoe and as soon as the lady far enough down the street Misty took off through the yard of the house she was in front of. She figured that if she hopped through yards she shouldn't have to hop no more than three or four gates until she gets to the main street. She prayed that she didn't run into any dogs. It took her about eight minutes to hit Brand Ln. She knew that if she made a right on Brand it would take her to Main St., and she remembered seeing and O'reilly Auto Parts right there, so she could go in there and call a taxi.

It took her about six minutes to get down to O'reilly. "Can I please use your phone to call a taxi. I am trying to get away from an abusive ex boyfriend and I don't have much time before he realizes that I am gone. Please." Misty cried in an urgent, child like voice, as she tried to catch her breath. "Yeah, here. Use my cell." The young hispanic guy said from behind the counter. "I will give you a ride if you need one sweetie. Free of charge." Said and older black guy who was purchasing a couple quarts of oil. "Oh my gosh, thank you. That is even better. I would appreciate that so much. I am not from here so I don't have anyone to call. I was just going to take a taxi to the airport." Misty cried, still trying to catch her breath.

"Thank you so much. I really need to get to the Bush airport. If you can't take me all of the way that is fine, and I will pay you even though you said free. I know that it is kind of far." Misty said when they got in the car. "No problem sweetie. I don't like to see young ladies in bad situations. I will take you all the way there. I just need to stop and get some gas. What's your name young lady?" He said. "Oh, where are my manners. My name is Misty. And yours?" She said. "Just call me Joe short for Joseph. I don't mean to pry but are you going to be able to get where you going once you get to the airport?" Joe asked with concern. Misty didn't like taking advantage of people, but she was hustler so it just came naturally when the opportunity presented itself. "I have no idea. I just know that I need to get back home to Los Angeles before this man kills me. I should probably call my dad, but I am not sure if he is going to have enough. Either way I will figure it out somehow. As long as I am away from that horrible man." Misty said in a sad and vulnerable voice. "How old are you sweetie?" Joe asked as he was checking out the curves that he could see. "I'm 19 but I will be 20 next month on the

3rd." Misty said, trying to sound gullible. "Uhm hmm, well I might be able to get you a ticket home." Joe said as he reached over and put his hand on Misty's inner thigh, just short of her crotch. "Oh my gosh that would be so nice of you. I would really, really appreciate that." Misty said.

Joe reached his hand a little further and began rubbing on the crotch area of Misty's shorts. Misty timidly moved his hand and asked, "What are you doing?" "You are going to have to show me how much you appreciate this." He said. Misty acted as if she was embarrassed and shy. "I think that I know what you mean, but I have only been with 3 men in my life, so I think that I will just take my chances and make some calls when I get to the airport." Misty said as she moved his hand. "I am so sorry if I made you feel uncomfortable. That is the last thing that I wanted to do." Joe said, feeling ashamed. "No, don't apologize. I understand and I would do it, but a ticket is only about $400 and to sell myself for so little….. I just don't think that I would be able to look at myself the same. I would feel cheap." Misty said.

Misty knew exactly what she was doing. She knew that he could afford at least a thousand. "I would never want such a beautiful young lady like you to feel cheap. How about this. If you would be willing to spend the night with me, we could book your flight online for tomorrow morning and I will pay for it with my credit card, and I have a printer so we can print it out so that you feel more comfortable,I will give you, saaaay, 1100 cash. How does that sound?" Joe proposed. "You might have to get me a bottle of wine to loosen up, but I am not in a position to turn that down. So, yes we can do that." Misty said. "I have lots of wine at my house. It is not too far from here. We will be there in about two to three minutes." Joe said in a pleasant and satisfied voice.

"Shit this worked out better than I thought it would." Misty thought to herself.

HOME SWEET HOME

"Hey Cuzz, what's up, can you pick me up from

LAX at 3:00. I'm coming in on United?" Misty asked as soon as she heard PB's voice through the phone. "You lucky I answered the phone cuz I didn't recognize the number. But, fo sho, I might be a little late though cuzz I got somethin' to do at two. Where you comin' from?" PB said. "Yeah it's a long story I had to grab a bulshit minute phone from the store. But yeah, I'm coming from Houston. But I will see you when I get there, because I just boarded the plane and I have to shut my phone off." Misty said. "Aight Baby, I'll see you in a lil bit." PB said. "Thank you, Daddy." Misty said, then hung up. "Damn, I should have bought another outfit before I got on this plane. I don't want him to see me in public like this. Oh well, fuck it." Misty thought to herself.

"What the fuck are you wearing? I know you

know better than to come out like that." PB said, as soon as Misty got in the truck. "Nigga, I wear what the fuck I wanna wear. Besides, I got into some shit and I had no choice. You see I ain't got no luggage." Misty said. "Damn, you don't have any. I didn't even realize that. What happened, what you done got yourself into this time?" PB said as he gave her a hug.

She felt good to be back around someone that she did not have to worry or think twice about. Misty loved going to new places and she got a thrill out of fucking with new niggaz, but sometimes she just needed the comfort of not having to worry. The comfort of unconditional love and security. As much as she plays the big girl tough role in the streets, she needs to be loved every now and then. If only just to recuperate and gain her strength back so she can get back in the streets with a level head.

"PB, I love you more than you will ever know. Now, what are you doing tonight? I got some money put aside just for a night wit you. Can I get that tonight?" MIsty said as they were hugging. "Uhh, I'm not sure yet. I'm gon have to let you know in a few hours. Ok, baby?" PB said. Misty knew that PB did not like telling her no so anything except a straight yes meant no. "Yeah, yeah, yeah, nigga just tell me you can't. Don't have me waitin on you and then you stop answering yo phone. I ain't got time cuzz I got a million other things that I can do." Misty said, with an attitude. "Fa real Baby, cuzz I really wanna spend some time wit you, I just have some business to handle." PB replied. "Ok, PB. Whatever.

Anyways, I need to buy a car ASAP." Misty said, already

blowing off the thought of spending the night with him.

"How much you tryna spend and what kinda car

you want?" PB asked. "I got 30 racks to cash somethin

out. I don't know what, I just want somethin fresh."

Misty said. "Shit, 30 racks. You fo sho gon have

somethin fresh. When you wanna get it?" PB said.

"Right now, if possible, but I know you on some other

shit so just hit me as soon as you ready to take me."

Misty said.

"Fo sho, Baby. Where you going right now?" PB

asked. "135th and Budlong, at Giz spot. I'm staying wit

him cuzz I ain't got no spot out here. You know I been

living in Vegas for the last few months. I got a nice place

out there. I would ask you to come visit but I know you

be full of shit so you just let me know when you ready."

Misty said. "I didn't know you was out there, I'm getting

ready to move out there soon." PB said. "Well, let me

know when you ready. You know I got you." Misty said.

"Yeah I know you got me Baby. But this what we gon

do. I ain't even gon have you sittin around like that.

Tomorrow morning I will pick you up at 9 and we gon go

get a whip. Aiight?" PB said. "Aiight that's what's up. PB

don't have me waitin please, you know I ain't got no

kinda patients." Misty replied. "Yeah, yeah I know, I got

cha don't trip crip." PB said.

They pulled up to Giz spot and PB put the truck

in park, got out, and walked around to the passenger

side. He gently grabbed Misty's chin and looked into her

eyes. "Look, I really need you to slow down. I love you

and one day I am going to take you out of these streets and give you what you deserve. But I need for you to stop playing wit these niggaz before somebody really hurts you. I be worried about you. Show me that you can settle down and be the woman that I need, have some patients, and in time I will be the man that you need. Do you understand Baby?" "I do understand, but what is the wait for? I know that you are sitting on at least 200K, I'm sitting on 75 so the way I see it is that we can do this together and have a nice life." Misty said. "Yeah, I hear you but I got a lot going on and I'm just not gon stop in the middle of things to settle down. You need to chill out though and stop fuckin wit these niggaz. Keep gettin money, keep stackin and wait for Daddy ta be ready for you. You claim to love me, you claim that we are perfect for each other, but your actions tell me that you don't really believe that." PB said. "And what do you think your actions tell me? You got a different bitch pregnant every other month. You got a home with another bitch but you tell me to wait on you. Nigga, don't play me. I am not one of those basic ass ghetto bitches that you fuck wit. You can't sell me that same dream that you are selling to those bitches. As a matter of fact we can just cut all this shit right here right now. I love you, I always have and I always will, but I know that we will never be because we are too much alike. Now just have yo ass over here at 9 so I can get a whip. And it's gon be fresher than yours." Misty said with attitude. "You somethin else you know that, but ok I will be here. You just have yo ass ready."

PB said, and then kissed her gently upon her lips.

FAMILY

Misty seen that the Benz was gone so she figured that Giz wasn't home. She went in the house, rolled a blunt, and soaked in the tub. As she was soaking in the tub she was observing the faint whelp marks that were still on her stomach from Shorty. "I wonder if I will ever be able to get these marks completely off of me." Misty said to herself.

Just then she heard Giz walk in the house. "Aye

Cuzz, I'm home. I'm in the tub right now. Be out in a minute." Misty yelled. Giz barged right in the bathroom as Misty was stepping out of the tub and gave her a big bear hug. He didn't care that she was naked and still wet. "What up Cuzzo, I missed yo lil wet naked ass." He said. "Nigga get yo crazy ass outta here so I can put some clothes on." Misty said as she was laughing and pushing him off of her.

"So what it does cuzz?" Misty said to Giz when she came out of the bathroom. "Shit just been in the studio and gettin to da bread as always. Worried about yo crazy ass." Giz replied. "I keep telling you that you ain't gotta worry about me Cuzz. I'm always gon be ok." Misty said. "Yeah, yeah, yeah you keep sayin that. But I'm always gon worry about you. And just like always, I got cha no matter what." Giz said "I know Cuzzo, and I love you for it." Misty replied.

"I would ask how Houston was, but knowing you I probably don't even wanna know, I'm just happy you made it back safe." Giz said. If he only knew the hell I went through out there he would be ready to blow up the whole damn city. Misty thought to herself. "It was cool, I went to Florida for a few days, too. I came back wit 30 racks so I would say it was successful run," Misty replied. Yeah a successful run through hell, she thought to herself. "Damn Cuzzo, you really be out here rackin up. I wish it was in another way, but shit I can't even be mad at you." Giz said. "Yeah Cuzz, it pays, but this shit is starting to take a toll on me mentally. I'm getting colder and colder by the day." Misty replied. "Well shit, I know you have to have at least 100 stacks put up, just stop doing that shit," Giz said. "And do what? Sit around and spend that shit up, then look around and I'll be broke. The way I spend money that shit would be gone in about a month, no longer than two. Besides, gettin money is embedded in me Cuzzo. I just can't help it. I love this shit. But, I'm about to go drop 30 on a whip in the morning. I don't know what I'm gon get yet, but I do know it's gon be fly." Misty replied. "Well, whatever you gon do what you want anyways, just be careful Cuzz. But what you really need to do right now is stop playin and roll sumtin up, can you believe I ain't smoked all damn day." Giz said. "Nigga you lyin." Misty said. "Yeah you right, I am lying. But shit it seems like it." Giz said.

MIsty and Giz smoked a couple of blunts and talked for a while. She really needed that. "Aye Cuzz, I'm gon shoot to ma Pops house for a little bit. I ain't seen him in awhile." Misty said. "Ok Cuzzo, fa sho. I'll be here. Or I might hit the studio for a bit. You gotta here this new track I'm working on called "Welcome To Gardena" you gon love it." Giz said. "That's what's up. I'm gon call you when I leave there and if you at the studio, I'm gon shoot through." Misty replied.

"Hey Honey." Germ said as soon as Misty walked through the door. "Hey, Daddy. I got us something to sip on. I missed you." Misty said as she walked to the kitchen to get two glasses. "You always got something to sip on. I'm starting to think you might be an alcoholic like me." Germ said and laughed. "Shit, I ain't no damn alcoholic, I just like to drink. You must be gettin old

sayin some shit like that." Misty shot back. "Old is a

mental state, one that I will never be in. I was waiting

for you to come by, PB told me he picked you up from

the airport. He also told me how you were looking. You

really need to chill yo ass down before you have me in

the penitentiary. I don't know what you got yourself

into out there, but it seems like I'm constantly hearing

shit about you in these streets. You don't even know

how many times being ma daughter has saved you."

Germ said in a concerned and serious tone of voice.

"Daddy, I ain't come over here to hear all dat. And

besides, I know how to handle myself in these streets. I

been doing it and not once have I had to call on you to

handle anything for me. I'm good. And I know you're ma

Dad, and I know you a street nigga so I know things get back to you. But trust me when I say I got this. And fuck all these niggaz, it wasn't your name that saved me. 90% of these niggaz is lame, wit no game, and couldn't fuck wit me if their life depended on it. And the other 10%, I just don't try them. I ain't stupid I know what niggaz to keep on ma side and I know what niggaz ain't a factor. It's yo blood that runs through ma veins, and I got every bit of savage in me that you got in you. The only difference is that you are a gangsta by title, and I'm a hoe by title. And I know that you hate hearing that but it is what it is. And I'm gon keep gettin ma money, and these niggaz gon stay mad, and I'm gon stay not giving a fuck.And if they try me, well then you already know exactly what you taught me to do." Misty replied with attitude. "I don't know what I created when I created you but I do know that yo ass better chill out. And I'm not gon go back and forth you either. And when's the last time that you talked to and seen your mother?" Germ asked. "Daddy, you already know how my mother feels about my lifestyle and as much as I love her, I just can't deal wit the lectures and judgements. That shit be having me fucked up in the head. And right about now you starting to sound just like her. You musta spoke to her." Misty said. "Yep, and she misses you, she's worried about you, and she wants to see you. Promise me that you gon see her before you leave again." Germ said. "Look Daddy, I'm bout to go. Tell my mother that I love her. And I love you, too. But, I really can't deal wit this right now." Misty said as she was grabbing her purse and keys and walking out the door.

Misty loved her mother, but they were never close. Growing up the block raised Misty and her mother was so busy being young and having fun that sometimes it seemed like she forgot she even had a daughter. By the time that she started growing up and being responsible Misty had suffered so much abuse and dealt with so many things on her own that it didn't really matter anymore, the monster was already created.

But Misty also knew that her mother didn't mean any harm and she would go around more, but unlike her father, her mother was judgemental, and even though Misty knew that her judgements were pure, out of love, and most of the time right she just didn't want t

WHEN DRAMA FROM THE

PAST CREEPS UP

"I'm gon be pulin up in 26 minutes, so be outside." PB said when Misty answered the phone. "Cool, I'm already ready and waiting on you." Misty replied.

"Aye, if you was any other bitch I would take yo 30 racks. Bring you a car for 10 racks, and pocket the rest." PB said when Misty got in the car. "I'm not even bout to play wit yo ass and the shit you be doing to yo stupid ass bitches. That's probably why you won't fuck wit me cuz you can't play me. But anyways, I know what I want. I want a new Infiniti G35 Coupe. And don't bring me to no bullshit ass lot, cuz I don't want a used car I want it brand new. I wanna smell the newness burning off the engine. Find an actual Infiniti Dealer." MIsty snapped back. "You sho got a lotta attitude, you better bring that shit down a notch. And you might wanna grab another 5-10 racks for that." PB replied. "I got 35K on me. And that should be enough. Cuz since I'm paying cash they gon give me a deal anyway, right." Misty said. "Yeah, they will. That should be good." PB said.

Three hours later Misty was leaving the lot with a brand new, wet black with chrome trim Infiniti G35 Coupe. "I'm proud of you Baby. You really out here gettin it how you should be. It's not many 23 year old bitches that can cash out a brand new whip like that, a fresh one at that. I knew you was grinding but damn, shit you damn near up there wit me." PB said as he gave Misty a big hug. "Thank you, Daddy. Maybe by the time you get to Vegas we can play big bank take little bank." Misty said playfully. "Hell nah, you ain't gon take ma lil change. But I was serious yesterday. You be careful and think about what I said and keep yo ass out the way." PB said as he looked in her eyes. "I hear you now, and I heard you yesterday. But right now, I'm about to go tear the mall up. I'll hit you later, or better yet, hit me when you wanna hook up. I love you." Misty said as she was getting into her first brand new car. She was so proud of herself. At this moment couldn't nobody tell her shit and nothing could steal her joy. Now it was time to hit the mall, but first to Sprint so she could grab a new phone.

Misty got back to Giz spot around around 6 o'clock, but he wasn't home. She was kind of disappointed because she wanted to show off her new whip. Oh well, he will just have to see it later. Now it's time to get to work and start replacing these racks I just spent today. She thought to herself. By 7:30 she was dressed and ready to go. She figured that she would match her new whip.

She had on a black, two piece mini skirt and backless shirt set, high heel, peep toe, Ferragamo boots with silver trimming, white gold accessories, and a black Ferragamo clutch. Now, usually she wouldn't wear such high end things on the track, but today she was feeling herself. She figured that she would take the drive to Anaheim and get down on Harbor until it was time to go to Hollywood. She hadn't been out there in a couple of years but from what she remembered it was popping.

Misty made it to Harbor around 8:45. There

weren't many hoes down but there were enough to know that it was open. She decided to play the Garden grove side of Harbor because that is where she seen the most hoes down at. Misty was down for just about 3 hours before the bullshit started.

"Say Bitch, you know who it is Drama The Mutha Fuckin P Hoe! You thought you got away, well think again Bitch cuz I'm on yo mutha fuckin heels tonight Hoe." Misty heard coming from a black Tahoe. "Om my fuckin God. Can I ever get away from these niggaz and just hoe in peace." Misty said to herself as she did an about face and went the other way. She had $680 on her and she was about a mile away from her car. And she had no doubt in her mind that Drama was going to hop out on her.

Drama was about 5'6", 160 lbs., kept a low fade, with a medium chocolate complexion. He was a Pimp that Misty met a couple of years back after her turn out folks, Redd went to the penitentiary. Drama and Misty was actually very cool with each other but this was the first time that she had seen him since she left. And at this point she had zero trust for any pimps and didn't put anything past anyone. She just wanted to make it to her car and get the fuck out of there.

Drama was in every other driveway, or side street that Misty approached. She was just waiting for him park and get out. She just hoped that she didn't scuff her $900 boots that she had been very careful in all evening long. Finally, she made it to the complex that her car was parked in. And just as she thought she was cool Drama jumped out of nowhere from behind her. "Hey Bitch! How you just gon leave me wit that punk ass bitch after me and you had an understanding, Hoe. I been waiting to see you ass." Drama spoke in a very low, but very stern voice.

Misty was not worried about anything that he was saying because when he jumped out from behind her, she lunged forward and one of her heels got caught and broke. She was so pissed that she couldn't help herself. Normally she would assess the situation. But at this moment she did not care that she was in a dark parking lot, with no one around, and that he could possibly really hurt her. "Nigga what the fuck is wrong wit you? I ain't never did shit to yo stupid ass. These are mutha fuckin $900 boots that you just made me break!"

Misty yelled as she was picking her heel up off the ground.

She didn't even make it all the way when Drama socked her in the back of her head, then snatched her back up by her hair, and pinned her against somebody's car. "See Bitch, I wasn't even gon put ma hands on you Hoe. I just wanted to get in yo mutha fuckin face and let you know some things. But Bitch you will never disrespect me. You think I give a fuck about some mutha fuckin boots Hoe." Drama exclaimed. "Fuck you, Drama. Let me the fuck go." Misty said with fire in her tone. Drama laughed a little, backhanded her, then pulled her down to the ground, and stood over her. Now his hand was around her neck, and Misty was laid on her back looking up at him. "Bitch you think this shit is a mutha fuckin joke. I will really hurt you about disrespecting me." Drama said. Then open hand slapped her but with the bottom of his palm.

Misty reacted and with the boot that was broke she managed to push him up, then she kicked him as hard as she could in his chest,knocking the wind out of him and he flew back. She already had her key in her hand, she grabbed her clutch that was right next to her, jumped up and ran to her car which was only about four parking spots away. She always backed into parking spots just in case she had to leave quickly, so by the time Drama caught his breath Misty was skirting off.

"I swear to God I am starting to hate these faggot ass Pimps more and more every fucking day! Broke ma mutha fuckin boot! And I don't even got the fuckin heel to get it fixed! This is exactly why I never wear good shit on the track, and the one time I make an exception this bull shit happens. Fuck that I'm gon back to get ma fuckin heel. Fuck I wish I had ma heat on me." Misty rambled on to herself. Just as she was about to hit the freeway she decided to go back and get her heel. Then she realized that she didn't have her gun so she turned back around and just got on the freeway and chopped it up as a loss.

Then to make things even worse, this is probably one of the only times that she didn't have her duffle bag with extra shoes and an outfit. So she couldn't even just go straight to Hollywood. So she headed back to Gardena in a horrible mood. Misty got back to Gardena close to 1:30. Giz was up writing raps. "What's good

Cuzzo? What kind of whip did you get? I gotta go see."

Giz said excitedly and he got up and headed to the door.

Misty handed him the key, "here Cuzz go check it out.

I'm pissed cuz I tripped and broke ma damn Ferragamo

boots. I'm about to shower and change real quick

before I head back out."

"Well at least I still got ma money." MIsty said to

herself as she was getting into the shower. She just took

a quick shower and threw something on so that she

could make it to Hollywood in time enough to get a

good run for the night. By the time she was done Giz

had a blunt rolled and in the air.

"Damn, you couldn't wait for me to light it up,

Cuzz?" Misty said with an attitude. "Look I ain't the one

that got cha panties in a bunch. And I just lit it anyways.

Here." Giz said as he passed her the blunt. "Thanks

Cuzzo, I really need this. I am so mad about ma boots."

Misty said. "Oh well, get over it. That mutha fuckin whip

is saucy. It definitely fits you." Giz said excitedly. That

brought Misty's vibe up a little bit. "I know right. Wait

until I throw the beat, rims, and tint on it. And ma

license plate gon say "FUPAYME" wait til I come back

out here from Vegas." MIsty said excitedly, almost

forgetting about her broken boots. "Yeah, that shits gon

be nutty." Giz said. "Yep. But ok Cuzz, I'm about to get

back to this money. I'll see you in the morning. Love

you." Misty said as she handed Giz back the blunt and

kissed him on the cheek.

ALL CRIED OUT

On the way to Hollywood Misty did her best to put herself in the right state of mind. But she did not have not one CD so it was pretty hard to do listening to the radio station. She kept thinking about how Drama made her break her boots and she was getting more and more pissed. "Fuck it I'm just gon take this shit out on these tricks tonight." Misty said to herself as she was riding down Sunset trying to figure out where she wanted to get down at.

She hadn't been down on Sunset since she shot Shorty. Not that it made her much of a difference, she was just hoping that it was still cool. Cuz as far as she could see it was a Saturday night and she hadn't seen not one hoe yet. Usually after something like that happens the track will get shut down for a while but she didn't think that it would be shut down for this long.

You know what, I'm just gon get the fuck outta L.A. again. Maybe I'll take a trip up to the Bay and see what that do for a while. But first, I'm gon shoot to Vegas and get ma heat. Misty thought to herself.

The next day she was on her way back to Vegas. She decided to give Lil Giz a call and let him know that she will be there in a few hours. Also to see if he wanted to go up to the Bay with her because it is super ruthless up there and she really didn't want to go by herself. "Hey stranger, I ain't talked to you in a bit." Lil Giz said when he answered the phone. "You know me, I be here, there, and everywhere. Movin too fast. But anyways I'm on ma way back to Vegas right now." Misty replied. "How much money you got, cuz I know you ain't call a Pimp to tell em you on the way wit out no money for em." Lil Giz said. "Here you go wit that bullshit. Look I don't want no fuckin Pimp, ok. But I thought you was a lil more than that so I called. But fuck it, bye." Misty said, then hung up. Lil Giz called right back. "What?" Misty said with attitude, when she picked up. "Look bitch, don't......." Click. Misty hung up again, this time, with no intentions on answering the phone again. Well, I guess I will be going to the Bay by myself. Misty thought to herself.

Misty got home around noon. When she walked

in Lil Giz was sitting on her couch, drinking the last of her Remy, and watching TV. She couldn't help but to let out a little giggle. "You know what, I'm not even bout to play wit you LG. Get yo ass the fuck up outta here." Misty said as she was putting her things down and heading to her room. Lil Giz just looked at her without a word then continued watching TV. Misty didn't even have the energy for him at the moment. She just went to her room and closed the door.

She came out of her room about a half an hour later and he was still there. "Damn, nigga didn't I tell you to leave? And how fuckin long have you been here? All ma damn juice, snacks, and liquor is gone.? Misty said. Visibly irritated as she looked in her fridge and cabinets. Lil Giz got up, set his empty glass on the counter and the empty bottle in the trash, and said, "I'll be back in a little while. Hopefully then you ain't got no punk as attitude." "NIgga, what the fuck you mean? You all up in ma shit like you live here. Gimme ma fuckin keys and get the fuck out!" Misty yelled. "You see, normally, I would beat a bitch up for talking to me like that. But, because I know you a lil off and touched upstairs I'mma give yo ass a pass." Lil Giz said playfully, attempting to lighten the mood. "I don't give a fuck what you normally do. Nigga, normally I would shoot a mutha fucka all up in ma shit without ma say so. Now gimme ma fuckin keys and get the fuck out!" Misty yelled again.

Lil Giz had a smirk on his face and his hands behind his back as he walked around the counter, and into the kitchen where Misty was standing. The closer that he got to her the more that she backed up until she was backed up against the refrigerator. "Listen to me and listen to me very carefully. I am not one of them punk ass niggaz that you deal wit. And not only have I been nothin but respectful to you. Bitch, I have been there for you when nobody else was. No before I knock yo faggot ass out would you like to try this shit again?" Lil Giz said in commanding tone. Misty took a deep breath. "Yes, you have been there for me, and no you haven't been disrespectful towards me. And you are definitely not a punk ass nigga. But I am far from a faggot and I told you to get out of ma spot and that is what the fuck I meant. I am not in the mood." Misty said as calmly as she possibly could.

Lil Giz turned around, walked to the couch, sat down, and patted the cushion next to him, then said, "Come 'ere. Have a seat. And this the last time I'mma be civilized wit yo ass." Misty closed her eyes, shook her head, and took a deep breath, then she went to sit down. "What Lil Giz? What is it that you want?" Misty said pleadingly. Lil Giz put his hand around her neck, not rough, but firm. He looked into her eyes, then said, "You. I want you." Then he kissed her deeply. Misty didn't have the strength to fight it. She didn't even know if she wanted to fight it. So she gave in to him. She let go of all of the tension that she had built up and gave herself to him.

He picked Misty up and carried her to her room, then laid her on the bed. He undressed her, then grabbed the baby oil off of her dresser, and massaged her entire body until she fell asleep. After she was sleep he got in the bed and held her until he fell asleep next to her.

A few hours later he felt her tossing and turning so he tried to hold her tighter, but she got up. "LG I can't do this with you. Thank you, but can you please leave?" Misty said softly. Lil Giz pulled her back down and close to him. "What you not gon do is keep runnin around and having me as your substitute Pimp. Ion know what happened to you. But I do know you was a good bitch. And I know you still are. And I'm done waitin. Last time I seen you I told you when I break you I'm breaking you for everything. And I meant that. And I wasn't just talkin bout money. You gon make a decision today. Either you fuckin wit me or you gon faget I ever existed. Cuz I can't do this wit you." Lil Giz spoke in soft but serious tone that let Misty know that he meant every word. Misty took a deep breath, pulled away from him, and got up. "I need to think." She said as she was walking into her bathroom.

She needed to wash all of the baby oil off and she wished that she could wash off the past year right with it. Lil Giz was right, she was a good Bitch. But she had been through so much and let down so many times that she turnt cold. She wasn't even sure if she was able to get back to who she was before. She just stood in the shower and let the hot water run over her, as she played back everything that transpired over the last year. Then she looked down at her body, and under the light that was in her shower she could clearly see permanent marks that Shorty left on her. She just dropped to her knees and cried.

Lil Giz heard her crying, he just sat there for a moment wondering if he should go comfort her or leave her to her thoughts and sorrows. He had a soft spot for Misty. They came from the same world, they were just alike. He needed to comfort her because it meant that there was still hope for him. So he undressed and joined her in the shower. "Baby get up." He said as he raised her up off of the shower floor and held her. If only the hot water that was raining down on their naked bodies could melt away the coldness that was settled on their hearts, they would both be ok.

He gently held her chin and raised her head up.

"Open your eyes and look at me. I got you. Stop fightin. Stop runnin. I'm not gon let you down." He said softly. Misty didn't say a word, she just hugged him as tight as she could and cried until she was all cried out. She realized that all of this time she was fighting trying to protect herself and she was the one doing the most harm to herself. She didn't want to fight anymore.

The water started getting cold. They got out of the shower and got back in the bed. They made love over and over again all evening, and all night long. When they finally fell asleep Misty felt like a huge burden was lifted up off of her shoulders. And she slept like a newborn baby.

IT'S TIME

It was after 2 o'clock when Misty finally woke up. Lil Giz was still asleep. Like usual she went to Starbucks. When she got back she sat at her dining room table contemplating the decision that she was about to make. She wasn't sure if she had anything left inside to give this man. Hell, she wasn't sure if she had anything left inside to give herself. For the last year of her life she convinced herself that no matter what she went through as long as she had money that she was happy. And she promised herself that no one would ever get close enough to hurt her again. She was done being used and she was done being a victim. But now this man has stepped in and made her feel again and she wasn't sure if she should trust him.

"Hey Mama." Lil Giz said as he walked in with a

smile on his face. "Hey LG, did you sleep good?" Misty

replied "Like a baby. I see you got your coffee. Where's

mine?" Lil Giz asked. "Shit, ma bad, didn't know you

wanted one. You wanna take ma new whip and go get

some?" Misty said with a grin on her face. "Aww shit

cuzz, you ain't tell me you gotta new. Where the keys

at?" He said excitedly. "They right there on the counter.

It's parked in ma spot. You should grab me some CD's

while you getting your coffee cuz I ain't got none."

Misty said as she pointed to the keys.

Lil Giz could tell that she was in deep thought

when he walked in. That's what he wanted her to do. He

wanted her to be completely sure about her decision

one way or the other. He knew that as a Pimp that he

probably shouldn't have the type of feelings for Misty as

he did, especially with the type of Bitch that she was. But he couldn't help it so today had to be the day that he was either going to have her or leave her alone for good. "Alright Mama, I'll be back in a lil bit. Is it any certain CDs that you want?" Lil Giz asked. "You know the type a shit I listen to." Misty said. Lil Giz was out the door.

While he was gone Misty did some dusting and straightening up up around the house while she was thinking. You know what, if any nigga is gon know how to really do right by me it gon be him. Fuck it, and if all fails I still got close to 40 racks still put up at Giz spot, and ma car is cashed out, so at least I won't be left wit nothing. She thought to herself.

She grabbed her phone and sent Lil Giz a text.

"Can you bring back a bottle of Remy, too please." She rolled two blunts, got her safe out of her closet and placed it on the coffee table. Then put on her blue and black laced panty and bra set, and her black satin robe. She put on Willie Hutch "I Choose You" but paused it so that she could hit play at just the right time. And waited for Lil Giz to return.

She could see her parking spot from the window in her living room, so she seen when he pulled. She ran back to her room and sprayed on some cotton blossom. "Here goes nothing. Back under instruction you go Misty." She said to herself. She greeted him at the door and took the Remy out of his hand. "Damn Mama, you needed a drink that bad." Lil Giz said. "Something like that. Can you set the CDs on the table, I will look at them later. But right now could you have a seat on the couch." MIsty said in a soft voice. "Will do" He replied.

When he turned around to walk to the couch he seen the safe sitting on table and the two blunts next to it. Then he noticed that the house was freshened up. And when Misty came from behind the kitchen counter with the two glasses of Remy and her robe undone, he noticed her, too. He couldn't hold back his smile.

"What you smiling for?" Misty asked playfully. "I know what I wanna be smilin fo, but wit the way you are I ain't to sure." Lil Giz replied. "I guess that's fair."Misty said, as she handed him his glass, then reached to hand him his blunt and grab hers, too. She set her glass down and lit both of their blunts, then picked her glass back up. They both took a puff then a sip. "So, you really think you can handle me, LG?" Misty

asked. "You gotta wanna be handled" He replied. MIsty

smiled. "So tell Mama, do you wanna be handled?" Lil

Giz asked. Misty looked up into his eyes. And for the

first time Lil Giz seen vulnerability "I think I might need

to be handled" Misty said softly. "You gon be aiight

Mama. Just tone down that slick ass mouth and you gon

fosho be aiight. You hear me?" Lil Giz said. "I hear you,

LG. And I believe you. I don't really know about toning

down ma mouth, but I know I'mma be aiight." Misty

said "Aiight Bitch, you can try me if want to. But we not

even gon get in all dat right now. What's up wit the

safe?" Lil Giz replied. "Oh, that's just there for show."

Misty said playfully. "Just fa sho huh? Well Bitch show

me da money. How bout that." Lil Giz popped back. "7-

27-7" MIsty replied as she nodded towards the safe, then pushed play on the stereo remote.

With "I Choose You" by Willie Hutch playing in the background Misty watched as Lil Giz counted out $63,750. She was so wet that her juices were dripping down her thighs. It had been a long time since she felt that feeling. That feeling that only a real hoe knows. To break herself to Pimp that has already shown that he is worthy and deserving of it. At that moment she fell back in love with the Game.

"Damn Mama, I knew you was gettin to it but I had no idea that it was to this extent. You gotta a nigga happy as a mutha fucka right now, real talk. A bitch ain't never really had me speechless but I really don't even know what to say. I figured you probably had like 10 maybe 15 racks put up. And you did all dis on yo own, imagine what you gon under instruction. And I'm gon let you know right now, as hard as you go by yo'self Bitch you gon go even harder fo me. This money right here, it's gon stay in this safe over here. Now you got a whole 'notha safe to fill up, and you still gon add to dis one, too. I'm cool, I'm ya patna, ya homeboy, and everything you wanna call me, but Bitch now I'm yo Pimp too and you ain't seen that side of me yet. Ain't no mo games from this point on. Ain't no mo doing what you want, when you want. Bitch you just chose up wit 63 racks. I gotta a real obligation ta you. It's ma job to make you even better and to do that I need to know that you gon listen and go against me." Lil Giz exclaimed as he was looking down into Misty's eyes.

Misty was on her knees in front of him taking in every word that he was saying. "Daddy, I'm wit you. I'm not gon go against you at all. I chose you for many reasons and I know that I made the right decision. And watching you count that money has me so wet that it's unbelievable. I don't think I ever been this wet in ma life. Please can you fuck me right now." Misty pleaded. "Stand up Bitch" Lil Giz demanded. Before he even touched her he seen her juices dripping through her panties and down her thighs. "Damn Bitch, take that shit off right now." He said. "Yes, Daddy" Misty said erotically.

They both undressed. Lil Giz grabbed her by her hair and forced her down on the couch and plunged into her like he was diving into a sea of pearls. Never had he been in pussy as wet and as tight as Misty's was at this very moment. "Damn Bitch is this what payin a Pimp do ta you?" He said in her ear. "Yes Daddy" Misty could barely get her words out. He had to pull out cuz it was feeling so good. "Hold on Mama, this shit feelin way too good." He said as he pulled out. Misty giggled, "What's wrong Daddy, you can't this good ass hoe pussy?" "Hell naw Bitch, I was damn near bout to cum countin day money. Then dis fire ass pussy on top a it. Ump ump ump. I fuck around and need some drugs to be able ta fuck you right now. I ain't even gon front." He exclaimed. Misty just fell out laughing. "You gon have ta work on dat cuz this pussy gon be super wet everytime I see you count ma trap. That's just what Pimpin do ta me." Misty said. "I'll tell you what Bitch, I'm gon go on ahead and finish fuckin you real quick. And you gon go add to dis dough. Then tonight, after you bring it in I'mma be ready fo you. Now bend dat ass over." Lil Giz said. "Yes Daddy, and I can't wait ta go get you some mo dough." Misty said. As much as Misty wanted to cum she preferred getting money on top of everything so she had no complaints.

For the next two weeks Lil Giz worked Misty everyday for 18 hours a day. From noon until 6pm Downtown, from 7pm until 1am on Tropicana, and from 2am until 8am on the Strip. She was making anywhere from 2K to 5K a day. Misty was happy with the results but she was starting to get very irritated from lack of sleep, and not being able to do the things that she enjoyed doing. She didn't even have time to smoke between shifts because Lil Giz didn't allow her to be high while she was working. She couldn't even have a drink while she was down. So she was sober the entire time.

He knew that she was getting irritated, that was his intentions. He needed to know that she was with him and that no matter how she felt she was going to follow instructions. And he planned on putting her through this for another month and a half before he eased up and allowed her to enjoy life again.

"Daddy, how long are you gon do this to me? I feel like I'm gon die. I need ta sleep. I need a blunt or at least a drink." Misty pleaded, on their way in. "A drink? So you ain't had drink in this whole two weeks?" Lil Giz replied. Misty didn't say anything. "Yeah Bitch don't say shit cuz I seen you get a few drinks. You want this shit to end, then learn how ta listen. You gon get a lil extra sleep today cuz we gon shoot to da land for bout a week or so." Lil Giz said. "Thank you, cuz I need a break so bad." Misty said. "You say dat like it ain't a thousand track fa you ta hit out there. And it's gon be all footwork, no hotels, since you like to sneak and drink." Lil Giz said. Misty took a deep breath. "You don't think you going over board? You act like I'm some mediocre ass hoe that you gotta keep down to get a decent trap out of. You really got me fucked up and I'm starting ta get pissed off, LG!" Misty exclaimed with a lot of attitude. He was waiting on it. He knew that attitude and that mouth was coming sooner or later. He was surprised that it took that long. "First of all BITCH, if you ever talk to me like that again I'm gon fuck you up.

Second of all, this is ma mutha fuckin program and

BITCH if I keep yo ass down fa three mutha fuckin days

straight den dats where ta fuck you gon be and you

betta not say a mutha fuckin word about it. Now you

either gon trust me n let me Pimp how da fuck I wanna

Pimp or you can get the fuck away from me and go back

ta being a faggot ass bitch n continue ta run ya head

into brick walls until yo funky ass looks up n you old,

lonely, and bitter wit nothin ta show but some mutha

fuckin clothes, cars, war stories!" Lil Giz said in a tone so

powerful that it sent chills up Misty's spine. "Fuck

yo……." SMACK! He reached over and slapped the rest

of her words right out of her mouth.

Misty was on fire and hurt at the same time. She

was so confused because she knew the Lil Giz really did care about her and had her best interest in mind. She just couldn't understand why he was treating her like this and why he was going so super hard on her. She expected him to go hard but she never would have imagined that he would take it to the extreme that he was taking it. She didn't know rather to ride it out or call it quits. On one hand she loved to be Pimped hard on, and on the other hand she hated to be treated bad. She just wanted him to ease up some and at least let her sleep and smoke.

When they pulled up Misty hopped out of the car before he could even put it in park and went up stairs and got in the shower. Lil Giz was feeling kind of bad because he knew what he was doing to her And up until now she hadn't complained not one bit. So while she was in the shower he rolled her a blunt and poured her a glass of Remy.

"Misty!" Lil Giz yelled, when he heard her getting out of the shower. She didn't even hesitate to come when he called. She was still dripping wet when she walked into the living room. "Yes, Daddy?" She said just a little bit of attitude. Lil Giz smiled inside because he knew that he had succeeded in bringing her back to being the obedient bitch that he heard stories about. Nevertheless, he was still going to continue on with his method of making sure that she was loyal and dedicated. "Hey Mama, after you finish drying off and all dat put sumtin comfortable on and come 'ere." He said. "Yes, Daddy" Misty said, then turned and went back into the room. She was out 5 minutes later in her basketball shorts and a wife beater.

She sat down on the couch next to Lil Giz. He handed her the glass of Remy that he poured for her, then lit the blunt and handed it to you. "Oh my God. Thank you Daddy. You don't even know how much I needed this." Misty said excitedly. She never thought in a million years that she would be so excited and appreciative over a drink and a blunt. Lil Giz just stared at her for a few moments. And she was relaxed enjoying smoking and sipping so much that she didn't even realize that he was staring at her. She had no idea how much she really amazed him.

He was going to talk to her, but decided to let her enjoy her relaxation while she had a chance. "I'm gon hop in da shower. Get you some things together so we can jump on this road in bout a hour. Don't even worry about clothes we gon get some when we get there just get everything else together, ma stuff too." Lil Giz said as he got up and walked to the bedroom. "Yes Daddy." Misty said pleasantly.

TRUST IS EVERYTHING

Misty slept the entire way to L.A.. Lil Giz didn't even speed because he wanted to give her a few extra minutes of rest. When they got there he pulled right up to the nail shop. "Here Mama, go on and get yo nails and feet done. Call me when you ready." He said. "Thank you Daddy." Misty replied. "You welcome Mama" He said a she was closing the door.

Lil Giz ran to the Galleria while Misty was in the nail shop and got her six complete outfits. Three pair of shoes, three jackets, three purses, and two outfits to match each set. And twelve panty and bra sets, because he knew that she liked to change those a couple times a

day, if not more. He spent about 5K, but was not

tripping not one bit. She deserved it all plus a lot more.

He only got himself two fits, a pair of shoes, and some

socks and drawers. He figured he didn't need much.

When he got back to the nail shop Misty was

standing outside smoking a cigarette, waiting on him.

"Let me see ya nails Mama." He said, as soon as she got

in the car. She got them money green, with LG on her

middle fingers. He smiled and said "That's dope."

"Thank you Daddy. I'm starving. I feel like I haven't

eaten anything in forever. "What you want Mama?" Lil

Giz asked. "Tam's, chilli cheese pastrami fries." Misty

answered super quick. "How bout Rick's?" Lil GIz

replied. "That's cool, they all bomb anyways. Please tell

me we going to Giz house. I miss ma cousin. And as hard as you been working me I feel like I need some family comfort." Misty said. LIl Giz laughed, "You need some family comfort Bitch?" "Yeah Nigga, I need some family comfort. I need ta rejuvenate, and regroup before you do me like that again." Misty said.

Misty's whole vibe changed once that got to Gardena. Lil Giz was cool wit that. She was a hood bitch at heart just like he was a hood nigga at heart. "Nigga huh? What happened ta Daddy. Bitch get in da hood and completely switch up on Pimpin." Lil Giz said. "Well, Nigga you betta catch up and flip yo hood switch on. You already know me." Misty shot back. "Is that right Bitch? Check this out, ma hood switch don't ever go off that shit's embedded in me. You just betta watch how many niggaz you call me and don't foget that I'm Daddy Hoe." Lil Giz said. "I don't see how I could ever foget that, but ok." Misty said. "As long as you know, we all good in da hood den." He replied.

"But look I wanna let you know that I'm proud a you. You did that two week run like soldier. You had yo lil issue this morning, but soon as I checked you you got back in line. I knew it was comin though so I was ready fo it. But I need you ta trust me completely. I need you ta know dat you ain't going hard fa no reason. I got some shit in da mix and I'mma really show you what you hoein fo. Just stay solid, stay down, n keep that mouth in check. You hear me?" Lil Giz said. "Yes, Daddy I hear you and you ain't gotta worry bout nothin. I ain't going nowhere. Trust me when I say, that I am tired of da Game spankin me." Misty replied. He just looked at her and nodded.

When they pulled up to Giz house Scrappe's car was parked in the front. "Is this gon be a problem fo you?" LIl Giz asked. "Fuck Scrap. I ain't worried bout dat nigga." Misty said with an attitude. "Bitch, that's not what I asked you. I know you ain't worried bout em." Lil Giz shot back. "No Daddy, it will not be a problem for me. As long as he don't say shit to me, about me, or referring to me in any way." Misty said with a slight attitude. "Aiight Bitch well, I'm gon tell you like this. I know you at home and you gon be you regardless. But if I gotta intervene, and I get into it wit ma big homie, cuz don't fo one second think I'm not gon have yo back over his. But if i get into it, have words, or anything of the sort I'mma beat yo mutha fuckin ass as soon as we step foot in our hotel room. Now do you understand dat.?" Lil Giz said. "And it will be a ass whoopin that I will gladly accept." Misty said. Lil Giz let out a sigh, "Oh boy. Bitch come on." He said as he was getting out of the car.

"What it does Cuzz?" Misty said happily, as soon as they walked in and she seen Giz. "What up Cuzzo? I wasn't expecting ta see you fo bout anotha month or so." Giz said as he gave Misty a hug. "What up Scrap?" Lil Giz said, reaching out to shake his hand. "What up Lil Homie? How you livin cuzz?" Scrappe said. "Shiiit, nigga havin it ma way and lovin it." Lil Giz said. "Yeah, I see." Scrappe said. "What up Mogwai? Da fuck you doing wit ma lil cousin. Dis look like some shit I should know about." Giz said to Lil Giz as he was shaking his hand and giving him a hug. "Cuzz, you already know. You knew when she first hit Vegas where she was gon end up. How could she not?" Lil Giz replied. "Aiight cuzz, well now I gotta tell you what I tell every nigga. I got her back no matter what and you betta take care of 'er Cuzz. Lil homie or not cuzz, that's ma fam." Giz said. "Don't trip crip. I got er just like you do." LIl Giz replied.

"Aye Scrap, Lemme holla at cha fo a sec outside ma nig." Lil Giz said. "What up Cuzz?" Scrappe said when he stepped outside. "I'm just makin sure we good ma nigga." LIl Giz said. "Why wouldn't we be. She a good Bitch I'on blame you fa snatchin er up. I rather see er wit you den one a dese fake ass niggaz she been dealin wit. Word of advice though you betta stay on er cuz dat bitch know how ta get ghost, quick. And dis da first place she gon run to. You betta empty dat safe she got in Giz room." Scrappe said. "Good lookin Cuzz. I got er though, she ain't goin nowhere." Lil Giz said as they were walking back in the house.

He didn't show it but Lil Giz was on fire inside. He wanted to snatch Misty by her fucking throat. But he decided to give her some time to tell him about the safe herself. Maybe she was going to surprise him with it. He was going to give her until 10 to tell him about it. And he didn't even want to think about what he was going to do if she didn't let him know about it. The cold part about it is that he didn't even want the money out of the safe, he just expected complete honesty and nothing less from her.

They all sat around and smoked, drank, played

dominoes, and talked for a couple of hours. Misty was so happy to be back at Giz house. It was a little after 7 o'clock and the more time that passed the more pissed Lil Giz got inside. He remained cool though. "Aye Mama, we gon leave here around 10 and head to a hotel so we can get some decent rest tonight and get on this money first thing in the morning." Lil Giz said to Misty. "OK, but I don't got no clothes, Daddy." Misty replied. "I went to da mall when you was gettin yo nails done. Trust me, yu good. I got you some fly shit." Lil Giz said. Misty smiled, "Thank you Daddy." He winked at her. Ok, so now she knows that we are leaving at 10. Let's see if she gon tell me bout the safe. Lil Giz thought to himself.

They put a few more blunts in the air. It was now quarter til 10 o'clock and Lil Giz was furious. Still he remained cool. "Aye we bout ta get up outta here in a few minutes so we can go catch some Z's." Lil Giz said. "Yeah, I am kind of tired." MIsty said. "Aiight Cuzzo, I love you and be safe." Giz said, as he gave MIsty a hug. "I love you, too Cuzzo. And I'm good now, no need to worry." "Aiight Mogwai, take care a ma lil cuzzo, and G safe." Giz said to Lil Giz. I'm gon take care of er alright. Lil Giz thought to himself. "I got er cuzz. We gon be back through here before we leave." LIl Giz said to Giz. "Aiight Scrap cuzz. I'll hit you up" LIl Giz said. "Aiight cuzz G safe, and remember what I said." Scrappe said to Lil Giz "I gotcha, good lookin on dat.' Lil Giz replied.

They were heading to the Renaissance near LAX, Lil Giz had already made reservations. His intentions were to enjoy an evening of relaxation with Misty and let her know how proud of her that he was. But now that has all changed. He thought that she gave him her all with no question, but to learn that she has a stash let's him know that she doesn't completely trust him, and that she is planning on them to fail. He will never admit it but he was hurt by that. He turned the music up so that he didn't have to speak on the way to the hotel.

When they walked into their room as soon as they set their bags down without a word Lil Giz slapped Misty with an open hand across her face, then another one, then another one. Every time Misty attempted to cry out Lil Giz slapped her again. Eventually his slaps turned into punches. Misty balled up in a fetal position on the floor directly in front of the bed and covered her face with her arms. Lil Giz blacked out as he landed punch after punch all over her body. When he came back to reality Misty was screaming at the top of her lungs.

Misty didn't know what was going on or why he snapped, and she was in so much pain that she couldn't even try to figure it out. She just wished that he would at least say something. But he didn't, he just kept pounding on her. She didn't know how much more of it that she could stand, until finally she just screamed, "Stooooooooooooop! Stooooooooooooooop!......." He stopped. He stood over her for a few seconds, then his only words were, "I thought you trusted me." Then he walked out the door. At that point MIsty knew exactly what was going on.

She laid on the floor crying for a few minutes.

Then managed to pull herself up and go to the bathroom. She knew that her face was ok because she had it covered during the worst of it, so she didn't even bother looking in the mirror. She got directly into the shower. She could feel the bruises all over her arms, her back and her rib cage, and a couple of knots on her head. She stood in the shower and cried for about an hour. When she got out he was still not back.

Although, she hated that he beat her up the way that he did. She completely understood why. She knew why she chose not to tell him about the safe. It was her security in case things didn't work out. Which meant exactly what he was feeling, that she didn't trust him. I gotta make this right. Misty thought to herself. She sent him a text.

When Lil iz left he drove around for awhile, then called Scrappe, "What up Cuzz, you still at Giz tilt ? I need to holla at you. I just fucked Misty up Cuzz." He said as soon as Scrappe picked up. "Nah I'm at ma spot. Is she aiight?" Scrappe asked. "I don't even know cuzz. I didn't even stay ta find out. But I'm on ma way." Lil Giz replied. "Aiight cuzz see you in a minute." Scrappe said, then hung up. Scrappe tried to call Misty and check on her but she didn't answered. He was kind of worried because he knew Lil Giz, but he knew that MIsty could take care of herself.

When Giz walked in he said, "I need some ice fa ma hands Loco." Scrappe looked at his hands and that made him more worried about Misty. "Aye cuzz you prolly needa find out if she cool." Scrappe said "I was so pissed cuzz I just blacked out ma nigga." Lil Giz said. "I already know how you get down cuzz, but you gotta remember who she is. I wanted ta kill dat bitch, but you gotta hold back when it come ta her. Giz gon trip the fuck out if find out so just be ready fa it lil homie." Scrappe said, not really knowing what else to say. Just then Lil Giz heard his phone go off, it was a text from Misty:

"Daddy, I apologize for not telling you about the safe. I have been through so much in this game that I felt like I needed to keep a little extra security. I do trust you. I trust you with my life. I made a mistake and I was wrong. Please forgive me and come back. The code to the safe is the same as the one at home. I don't care about that money. You have managed to break me out *of all of the faggot habits that I picked up on and that safe was the last one. I'm sorry, Daddy. P.S. Can you please bring me some epsom salt so that I can soak before you put me down."*

"This her right here. She cool. I'm bout ta go back and talk to er. Good lookin though cuzz. I'mma hit you up." Lil Giz said to Scrappe after reading Misty's text. "Aiight lil homie, I hope everything aiight." Scrappe said as they were walking to the door.

When Lil Giz made it back to the room Misty was in the bed sleep. He pulled the cover back and he could see the bruises all on her arms and both sides of her body. In a way he felt bad, but in a way he felt like she deserved it. He just got in the shower himself, then got in the bed next to her and went to sleep.

Misty woke up around 5am and she felt like she had been hit by a truck. She seen the epsom salt sitting on the table so she ran herself a hot bath and soaked. So much was going through her mind. She didn't want to leave Lil Giz, but she also didn't want him to think that it was ok to hit on her like that. Then at the same time she completely understood why he did it. Fuck it, I'm just gon ride it out and hope that we can get past this. Misty thought to herself.

When Lil Giz woke up he heard Misty in the tub. He was still upset with her but he knew how much she had been through so he tried to understand why she didn't tell him about the safe. At the same time trust was a big deal for him and she needed to know how serious he was about it. He rolled two blunts and went in the bathroom.

He lit his blunt then handed Misty her blunt and the lighter, and sat on the counter directly across from the tub. "You know you fucked up my trust, right," he said as he hit his blunt. "Yes Daddy, all I can say is that I'm sorry and whatever I have ta go through to make it up to you I will." Misty pleaded. "Look Bitch, I know you been through a lot, but I'm gon need you ta let all dat go and really gimme yo all. I don't even care that you had the safe out here. I'm just pissed cuz you didn't tell me bout it. Dat shit can stay right where it's at fo all I care. We not gon talk about dis no mo, but Bitch don't ever keep nutin from me again. Now, hit dat blunt one mo time and put it out then get yoself together. We gon go eat, then you gon get to it." Lil Giz explained to

Misty. "Yes, Daddy" was all Misty said.

BACK TO BEING PIMPED ON

Misty thought he had her ass down in Vegas. They were in L.A. for a week and it seemed like the only rest that she got was when they were driving from on track to the next. They hit Figueroa, Century, Sunset, Western, Sepulveda, Raseda, Lincoln, Harbor, Holt, and Long Beach Blvd. Misty stayed down anywhere from 6-8 hours on each of them. Whenever Lil Giz seen that she was too tired he would get a room and let her get 3-4 hours of sleep, take a nice shower, go sit down and eat, then she was right back down.

Misty was cool with staying down but she was getting irritated because she didn't feel like the money that she was making was adding up with the hours that she was down. And she was ready to leave L.A.. "Daddy, how much longer are we gon out here. I don't feel like I'm makin enough dough. I mean the numbers are adding up nicely but I'm workin way to hard. I was makin double, triple, and sometimes even more than that in Vegas." Misty complained. "I know Mama. We gon get outta here in the next day or so. But we gon hit Oakland befo' we head back home." Lil Giz said. "That's cool, when I called you when I was on ma way back ta Vegas I was actually gon ask you would you go to da Bay wit me. I heard that tracks is crackin up dere, but them niggaz be super trippin." Misty said. "Yeah, dey do be on one up there. I'mma see if Baby Giz wanna roll wit us. We gon hafta take ma whip though cuz yo shit too small." Lil Giz replied.

So now the plan was to ride back to Vegas, switch cars, pick up Baby Giz, then head to Oakland. Misty was cool with that especially since that would give her time to get some much needed sleep. When they got back to Vegas they went straight to Lil Giz apartment, Baby Giz was there packed and ready to go with his girlfriend Lala, that he finally convinced to get down for him. Misty had only met Lala a few times, she reminded her of her best friend Summer. She was about 5'5", light skinned, green eyes, a petite body, and hood as fuck.

"What up Lala?" Misty said. "What's up Bitch, I'm finally ready ta get dis wit you." Lala said enthusiastically. "Is that right?" Misty replied. "Hell yeah, BG told me how much money you be makin, and bitch I'm ready." Lala exclaimed. "Aiight, its time ta

show n prove then. This shit ain't easy but its worth it.

Just be ready ta stay down if you workin wit me. Cuz

Bitch LG keeps me down." Misty replied. "Don't trip Sis,

she ready and she bout ta be down right wit you." Baby

Giz jumped in and said. "I hear you Bro, but you already

know how fast ma hoein is. I hope she ready cuz I ain't

gon let er slow me down." Misty said. "Bitch you betta

not let a mutha fuckin thing slow you down when it

comes ta ma dough." Lil Giz said. "Don't trip, she

ready." Baby Giz said.

Misty followed Lil Giz into the bedroom. "Daddy,

I don't know if it's a good idea ta be trynna break her in,

in Oakland."Misty said. "Bitch that's on them. If you can

help er wit out fuckin up ma money den do so. Other

then dat, she gon sink or swim." Lil Giz replied. "Okay. Well, are we going to my spot? Cuz I wanna get a whole different wardrobe fa Oakland" Misty said. "Yeah, I know Mama. We gon stop by dere. I'm almost ready. You know I don't need a lot. But aye, how many cases a shells you got fa ya piece. Cuz gotta be ready fa anything going out dere." Lil Giz said. "Shit I only one case, Daddy." Misty replied. "Aiight we gon stop and get all dat cuz BG need some, too." Lil Giz said. "Sounds like a plan." Misty said as she was walking out of the room.

"Hold up Mama. Shut da do' and com'ere." Lil Giz said. Misty did as she was told. "Clothes off. Now!" Lil Giz demanded as he took his pants off. Misty got undressed as fast a she could, got on her knees, and waited for him to feed her. While he pushed himself inside of her mouth she opened up as wide as she could, allowing him to penetrate her throat; just how she knew he liked. She could barely breath, but in this moment his pleasure meant more to her than her own breath. He wrapped her hair around his hand, pulled her up and bent her over his bed. He took no mercy on her tight womanhood as he forced himself inside of her as hard as he could.

"Bitch, you gon keep gettin ma dough like you do?" He asked as he stroked her deep and hard. "Yeeeeeessss!" Misty yelled. H smacked her ass hard, and she let out a high pitched moan. "You gon stay down about mines, Hoe. All day and all night Bitch." Lil Giz demanded. "Yes, Daddy. I'm gon get yo money, I promise." Misty moaned. "Oh, I know dat Bitch. You ain't got no mutha fuckin choice, Hoe." Lil Giz said as he pounded her insides, pulling her back onto him by her hair. "Turn around Bitch, I want you ta look at me while you cum on dis dick." He demanded, as he released her hair from his grip.

Misty loved when he fucked her like this. He put his hand around her throat and gave her slow, deep strokes. With every stroke he could feel her pussy getting tighter around his dick. It never ceased to amaze him how good her pussy was. "Cum Bitch. Now. Show me dat I control you Hoe. Cum right now, Prove to me dat you mines." Lil Giz demanded as he went even deeper. "Daaaaadddyyyy, I'm, I'm, I'm cuuuuuuummmmmmiiiinnnnnn!" Misty screamed. He could feel her grip getting tighter and tighter, and as she came her pussy pulsated on his dick and brought him to his peak. He began fucking her deeper, harder, and faster. And just as he was about to explode inside of her he pulled out, snatched her down by her hair, and shot it all over her face. Then they both got in the shower and got ready to go.

When they got to MIsty's apartment Misty and Lala went up stairs while Lil Giz and Baby Giz went to the gun shop to get some shells. "Damn MIsty, yo place is fly as fuck. I want dis type a shit too. You gon hafta teach me how ta get it like you do." Lala exclaimed. "Girl, I stay down, I stay at it, n I stay askin fo it, no matter what. It's only so much I can teach you, you gotta want it n you gotta be ready ta risk it all ta get it. This shit ain't easy. So if you lookin fo a easy way out, this ain't it. I done been raped, robbed, beat up, in jail, alone, scared, n ma back against da wall on numerous occasions. I got through it all, wit some ta show fo it." Misty explained. Misty was a realist and she didn't believe in selling a dream to get a bitch to hoe. In Misty's eyes if you couldn't deal with the bad parts of the Game then you're not even capable of making it to the good parts of it. "I'm ready. Ain't shit gon stop me from gettin to da top." Lala replied. "We'll see." was all Misty said.

When Lil Giz and Baby Giz got back Misty and Lala was standing outside waiting for them. "You ready fo dis next run Mama?" Lil Giz asked Misty as they were pulling off. "I stay ready Daddy. You know you ain't even gotta ask me dat." Misty replied. "That's right Bitch." Lil

Giz said. "You hear dat Lala? I need you ta take notes from Sis. Cuz dats exactly what I ecpect outta you." Baby Giz said to Lala. "I know, I was just tellin her in da house dat I'm ready." Lala replied. "We'll see." Baby Giz said. "I had the exact same reply Bro Bro." Misty looked back at Baby Giz and said.

They jumped on the 15 S to the 5 N and 8 ½ hours later they were arriving in Oakland. It had been almost a complete day since Giz checked a trap from Misty and he was ready to put her down immediately. He had no doubt that she would be alright figuring things out on her own. But since they had Lala too, he didn't want to put the responsibility of teaching her and learning a new at the same time on Misty. So, they dropped Misty and Lala off at the Motel 6 on Edes Ave and went out to explore the track and surrounding areas.

They were back about two hours later. Lil Giz called Misty and told her to bring Lala and come down stairs. They grabbed something to eat from Wendy's while Lil Giz gave them the rundown. "Aye BG, tell yo Bitch to listen and observe carefully so she'lll know what to do when they split up." Lil Giz said. Baby Giz looked at Lala and she nodded to let him know that she was paying attention.

"Right now we on Fruitvale & E-14. E-14 is the track. You gon work between here n 39th. We gon drive down a couple a times so you can check it out, and hit a few back streets so you can get a idea of where you gon take ya cardates. We in a new city, and its a lil rowdy out here, so I need ta know where ta find you at all times. The trick room I want you ta use is on 38th n MacArthur. We gon ride down dere in a second." Lil Giz instructed. "I got it Daddy, a track is a track, I'm good. I'm just ready ta get down." Misty said. She was slightly irritated because she didn't like to be told where and how to hoe. There were a lot of times that she ventured away from the track. She went where the money carried her to. "Look Bitch if I was comfortable just droppin yo ass off wit out specific instructions den I woulda kicked yo ass out as soon as we got off the freeway. Just fuckin pay attention and do what the fuck I say." Lil Giz shot back. Misty took a deep breath, "Yes Daddy." She said with an attitude. "SMACK" Lil Giz backhanded her. "Bitch I'm not gon play wit yo ass out here. Now, we on

E-14, comin from 39th, make a right on 38th, Macarthur is bout a mile n a half ta two miles down. This the route I want you to ta take to da trick room." Lil Giz explained.

He wanted to slap the shit out of Misty again because she was picking at her nails and not paying attention to the surroundings like she was supposed to be doing. "Aye Bro, is yo Bitch payin attention cuz she might hafta get dropped off first and meet up wit dis Bitch after I beat er mutha fuckin ass, cuz she think this shit a game." Lil Giz said. "Maaaan, come on Sis, pay attention don't piss dis nigga off already." Baby Giz said. "Don't say shit Bro, she gon learn, da hard way." Lil Giz said as he backhanded Misty again. "Damn, I'm payin attention." Misty snapped. "Yeah ok, this MacArthur you gon make a right and dere da trick room go right dere on the left. This the way you gon get to n from dis room to da track. Now let me hurry up and drop ya'll off before I really hurt this Bitch." Lil Giz exclaimed.

Misty did not care about being slapped and she did not care about him being mad. She was ready to get down, but she had to go through all of this extra green, babysitting ass bullshit because of another niggaz bitch and it irritated the fuck out of her.

SHIT GETS RAL IN THE BAY

"Aiight Lala, this how we gon do dis. You gon go wit me on ma first three dates n after dat we gon separate. If you pay attention ta everything I do you should be fine. Lil Giz want us ta stay in this immediate area cuz niggaz be trippin up here n shit can get dangerous real quick. I'm sure BG told you bout stayin in pocket, please stay in pocket. I'm gon let you know off top if you get outta pocket around me not only am I leavin you on yo own, I'm tellin. So let's get ta dis money." Misty exclaimed as they were walking down 39th towards the track.

Hoes were down and Pimps were out. Misty really did love this shit. Those first three dates came quick, back to back. The first two were $100 car dates, and the last one had 250 for an hour so they went to the room. By the time they left the room Misty convinced him to spend another $150 to date Lala, too. When they got back to the track Misty asked Lala if she was ready. "Yeah, I'm ready. I just seen you get $450 in two hours. Hell yeah I'm ready." Lala said excitedly.

Just as Misty was about to tell Lala happy stacking, and be safe she thought that she seen Chaos drive by. She thought it was him because it looked like the same white Cadillac truck that he had when she fucked with him. Lala seen that Misty got kind of concerned, "You cool Misty?" Lala asked. "Yeah, I'm straight, I just don't feel like dealing wit Pimps right now. But ok Bitch, Happy Stackin, and be safe out here. You got ma number if you need me." Misty said as she started to cross to the other side of the street.

"Fuck, I hope dat wasn't Chaos." Misty said to herself. Misty knew the best way to avoid bullshit was to stay on dates, so for the next three hours she was on dates back to back. She didn't care how much the trick had, as long as they had $50 or better she was taking it, just because she didn't want to be seen. When she got off of her last date she seen the truck white Cadillac truck again, this time it slowed down when as it got closer to her. As the truck got closer to her she turned around with her face facing in the opposite direction of the truck and walked in the opposite direction of traffic, so that she could see what was coming towards her.

As Misty approached 33rd Ave. she seen Lala, "What's up girl how you doing out here?" Misty asked. "I ain't never made dis much money, dis quick in ma life. Bitch, I got $700!" Lala said excitedly. Misty wanted to be excited for her but she seen the white Cadillac truck approaching again, but from the opposite direction. At the same time there was a trick making a right onto 33rd Ave. "That's what's up girl, dats real good. But lemme go see what's up wit dis trick." Misty said as she was walking off trying to get outta sight before Chaos noticed her.

It all happened so fast. Chaos made a quick left

in front of traffic, threw the truck in park and him and two other niggaz hopped out. The trick pulled off before Misty got a chance to get in. "Lala call Lil Giz! Tell em it's Chaos!" She screamed as she started running. Chaos hopped back in the truck, while the other two chased her. Misty heard a shot, felt a surge of pain in her leg then fell to the ground. They snatched her up and threw her in the truck.

Lala was running behind them and seen everything happen. She called Baby Giz hysterically. "I don't know what happened Misty got shot, they got er!" Lala cried into the phone. "Wait bitch slow down. What da fuck you just say? Where ya'll at?" Baby Giz yelled back into the phone. "They got er Daddy, dey took er!" Lala cried. "Where da fuck you at bitch?" Baby Giz yelled. "33rd I'm on 33rd, hurry up please, dey shot er. Daddy, dey took er. Dey took er.!" Lala sobbed. Lil Giz was looking at Baby Giz waiting for him to tell him what was going on. "Aye cuzz get ta 33rd right now, Misty got shot and this bitch keep sayin dey took er. I don't know what da fuck is going on!" Baby Giz yelled. Lil Giz heart dropped to his stomach and he smashed down E-14 as fast as he could without saying a word. They turned on 33rd and drove down until they seen Lala standing in the middle of the street crying.

Lil Giz jumped out of the car. "Where da fuck is Misty at? What happened?" He yelled. "Dey shot er and gey took er Lil Giz. I tried to catch er but I couldn't." Lala cried. "Who shot er, who took er?" Lil giz asked hysterically. They heard sirens. "Aye cuz gettin da car.

Let's go." Baby Giz yelled. "Nah cuzz, fuck dat. Bitch stop cryin and tell me who got ma bitch." Lil Giz yelled at Lala. "Lala gettin da car!" Baby Giz yelled as he pushed Lil Giz in the passenger seat and jumped in the driver seat and pulled off. "Which way dey go?" Baby Giz asked Lala. "I don't know where dey went." she tried.

Baby Giz parked. "Look, I need you ta calm down n tell us what happened." He looked back and said to Lala. Lil Giz was in the front loading his gun. "We was on da corner. She walked up to a trick car. Den a white Cadillac truck pulled up and three niggaz hopped out. The trick took off MIsty ran. One of the niggaz got back in da truck and the other ones chased er. She yelled out to call Lil Giz and that Chaos did it. Then I heard a shot, she fell, dey grabbed er and threw er in da truck." Lala said as she was crying. "Remember dat nigga on da strip dat we beat up cuz he snatche er up. Nigga dat was Chaos, some lame ass nigga she used ta fuck wit." Lil Giz said. "Aye cuzz, we gotta find dis nigga." Baby Giz said.

"Yeah Bitch, you fucked up comin to ma town after da shit you pulled in Vegas. Did you really think you was just gon come out here n nutin was gon happen to yo faggot ass. Yeah just wait til we get to da spot bitch, you think you in pain now" Chaos said to Misty as he was driving. "Fuck you Chaos!" Misty yelled. "Aye nigga, dis bitch bleedin all over da place, hurry up n get ta where we going." One of the other nigga said. "Nigga shut up, didn't nobody tell yo stupid ass ta shoot da bitch. Find sumtin back dere ta wrap dat shit up." Chaos yelled. "Nigga don't mutha fuckin touch me! Cuzz, I swear ta God you gon die." Misty snapped. Her adrenaline was going so she didn't even feel any pain. She started socking the nigga that was on the right of her and trying to get to the door handle. Then she felt a surge of pain and everything went black.

"Bitch wake the fuck up!" Misty heard as she was coming to. Then she felt him kick her in her stomach. She couldn't tell where she was but she knew that she was outside. "Fuck you nigga, kill me." Misty cried out. "Don't worry bitch, I am." Chaos said in a cold voice. Then he kicked her over and over again going back and forth from her face to her stomach. "Aye nigga dats enough waste dat bitch n let's go." One of the niggaz said from the truck. Chaos shot her two times and hopped back in the truck and pulled off. One of the niggaz threw her purse out of the window as they pulled off.

Lil Giz and Baby Giz were driving all around Oakland looking for her. Both of them had their guns locked and loaded in their laps. Lala was in the back seat crying as quietly as she could. No one said a word. The sun started coming up and there was still no word from Misty or no sign of Chaos. "Bro bro, you gon hafta call Giz and get ere'body out here," Baby Giz said in a low voice. "You don't think I know dat, cuzz. We just need ta find ma bitch!" Lil Giz snapped. Baby Giz drove back to the Motel 6. "What da fuck you comin here fo. She damn sho ain't in da mutha fuckin room!" Lil Giz yelled. "Look Bro, I wanna find er just as much as you do, but we really need ta get nigga out here. We don't know what the fuck we dealin wit, cuzz." Baby Giz said. They all walked into the room without a word.

LIl Giz phone rang, it was a 510 number. He answered as fast as he could, "Hello!" "Hello this is Detective Roderick Brown from the Oakland P.D." The voice on the other end said. "Yeah" was all Lil Giz managed to get out. "I am trying to get in touch with the family of MIsty Green. Your number was the last one on her recent calls. She was involved in an incident. She is alive, but she is in intensive care at Highland Hospital……" Lil Giz hung up the phone. "She in intensive care at the hospital cuzz, dat was a detective." Lil giz yelled as he grabbed his keys and headed out of the door. Baby Giz and Lala followed him.

"Aye Bro, I know you wanna go up dere, but if

that was a detective….” Lil Giz cut him off, “Cuzz dis is ma Bitch, she not just some random ass hoe. Fuck dat mutha fuckin detective.” “I got you Bro.” Baby Giz replied. Lil Giz pulled by the front office and ran in and got directions to Highland Hospital. Fifteen minutes later they were pulling up to the emergency room. “I’m looking for Misty Green, she was brought in last night.” Lil Giz said to the lady at the front desk. She looked her up then called the unit that she was in. “She’s in surgery right now, sir. But I can direct you to the waiting area.” The nurse told him. Lil Giz almost dropped to his knees, but Baby Giz pulled him up. “Please Ma’am can you show us to the waiting area.” Lala said.

Lil Giz was pacing the floor when a detective walked in. “Are you the family of Misty Green?” He asked. "Yeah, you don't look like a mutha fuckin doctor, can you tell dem mutha fuckas ta hurry da fuck up!" Lil Giz snapped. Baby Giz jumped up and signaled to Lala to get Lil Giz then spoke to the detective. "Look, that's ma brother and Misty is his girl. We were lookin fo er all night then he got your call saying that she was here. We don't don't know what da fuck happened. Can you please tell us somethin?" Baby Giz said. "From what we can know. She was beaten, shot three times, and left for dead. We have an eye witness that heard gunshots, then seen a white truck pulling out of an alley sporadically. They went to see what happened, seen her laying there and called 911." The detective said.

Lil Giz heard everything that that the detective said. He pulled himself together and stepped in between the detective and Baby Giz, "I suggest you find the mutha fucka dat did dis befo I do. And we don't know shit dats gon help you. Now can you get da fuck outta here, cuz we ain't got shit ta say." Lil Giz said in a very cold tone. The detective knew that they weren't suspects so instead of increasing the hostility, he just handed Lil Giz a card and said, "Call me if you think of something." and walked away.

A GANGSTA FIRST

About an hour later a doctor came out and said, "Is the family of Misty Green here?" They all walked up to him. "Please tell me she ok." Lil Giz pleaded. "She's going to make it. But she is in pretty bad shape right now. I removed a bullet out of her right thigh, and one out of her right shoulder. Another grazed her head. She has multiple broken ribs, her nose is broke, and her jaw is fractured. We will need to keep her here for a few days under observation. But she is a very lucky lady, none of her injuries are life threatening, so she will be able to make a full recovery at home." The doctor said. Lil Giz sat in the seat behind him and cried like a baby. Lala hugged him. "When can we see er?" Baby Giz asked. "She's in recovery right now. She will be moved to a room within the hour and you are all welcome to see her." He replied. "Thanks Doc." Baby Giz said, as he shook his hand.

For the next two days Lil Giz never left Misty's bedside. She was sleep most of the time because of the meds that they were giving her. Baby Giz and Lala were back and forth from the room to the hospital. "Hey Bro Bro, has she woke up yet?" Baby Giz asked Lil Giz quietly when he walked in the room. "Nah, not really. They keepin er sedated for the most part. And when she do wake up she so outta it, she don't even know what's going on. I hate ta see er like dis Bro." Lil Giz said. "I know, I do too. But don't you think you should call Giz n Germ and let em know what's going on wit er?" Baby Giz asked. "She ain't gon want nobody ta see er like dis

Bro, she got too much pride. They say she gon recover,

so nah. I ain't tellin dem. I just wanna bring er home.

Get er situated. Did you find out where dat nigga be

at?" Lil Giz said. "I hear you Bro, n its yo call, but I think

you owe it ta Giz ta let em know. I did call Scrappe

though. He on his way out here. He say he gotta few

patnas up here dat can point us in da right direction.

You stay wit Misty though, I got dis." Baby Giz said. "I

gotta murk dat nigga maself cuzz. Look at what he did."

Lil Giz said as he pointed to Misty. "Aiight Bro, when

Cuzz get here we gon come get you, and leave Lala up

here wit Misty." Baby GIz said. Lil Giz just nodded.

    That night Scrappe made it out there a little

after 10 and met them at the hospital. "Aye cuzz, I'm

sorry dis shit happened. But lets find dis nigga n make it

right. Ma patna say he don't know too much about da nigga. But da nigga Chaos just knocked em fo one a his hoes bout a week ago. Da hoe live on 98th Ave and Lyndhurst, in some apartments right next to a mini mart. I think dats da best bet. He ain't gon expect nobody ta be lookin fo em dere." Scrappe said.

They sat across the street from the building for not even 15 minutes before they seen his truck pull in the parking lot. Lil Giz hopped out and walked calmly but fast across the street. Baby Giz was right behind him. Scrapped pull in and backed his car in two spots away from the truck.

As Chaos got out of his truck Lil Giz ran up on him put the pistol to his head. And just as he was about to pull the trigger visions of Misty in that hospital bed popped in his mind. He hit him in the head with the

pistol. Chaos fell to the ground. Lil Giz blacked out and

pistol whipped him until Baby Giz stopped him. "He

dead bro, lets go." Baby Giz said as he was pulling LIl Giz

to da car. Lil giz paused, turned around, and shot him

three times, all head shots. "Now dat nigga dead." He

said. They jumped in the car and pulled off.

"Take me back to da hospital." Was all Lil GIz

said. "Aye Bro, I know you wanna go right back, but you

need ta hop in shower and change outta those clothes.

So let's go to the room first." Baby GIz said. "Yeah, cuzz

he right about that. Gimme da clothes n da heat and I'm

gon get rid a dat shit. Den ya'll go back to da hospital

like all you did was go wash up and come back. I'm gon

jump back on da highway right now." Scrappe said. So

that's exactly what they did.

They weren't gone from the hospital for no more than an hour and a half. And Lil Giz was right back at her bedside. He felt relieved that the person who put her here was dead. But it still hurt him to see her like this. He just wanted to bring her home and forget all of this ever happened.

Misty was in the hospital for a week before the doctor discharged her. And the moment that she got discharged the detective was right there waiting. "Miss Green, would you mind coming down to the station and giving a report. It won't take long. We just want to find who is responsible for doing this to you" He asked. "It ain't nutin I can tell you ta help. I don't remember shit. Now if you don't mind all I wanna do is get outta dis bullshit ass city and go home." MIsty replied. Lil giz nodded at the detective and rolled Misty to the car, where Baby giz and Lala was waiting to help her in.

"You know I gotta kill dat nigga, right?" Misty said to Lil Giz as they pulled off from the hospital. "You just need ta rest an get better, Mama. That nigga is already handled." Lil GIz said. "Yeah Sis, you gotta get better." Baby Giz said. "I wanted ta do it." Misty said. Baby Giz and Lil Giz looked at eachother in the rearview and didn't say a word. Eight hours later they were back in Vegas.

"Do you need anything Mama?" Lil Giz asked. "Ummm actually Daddy, I do. But you gotta promise not ta laugh at me." Misty said. "I ain't gon promise, but I'll try." Lil Giz said. "The night everything happened. After ma last date, I tied ma trap up in a condom and stuffed it. I think it's still there. And I think I need you ta get it out." Misty said embarrassingly. "Are you fuckin serious?" Lil Giz laughed. "See, I knew you was gon laugh." Misty said. He got it out. "You have got ta be da only hoe in da world that gets kidnapped, beat up, and shot three times, and still got er trap. I don't even know what ta say." Lil Giz said.

For the next month Lil Giz and Misty stayed in her apartment and he nursed her back to health. He literally never left her alone and he did everything for her. "Good morning Mama, you sleep well? I think that maybe today we should get outta the house for a bit." Lil Giz said to Misty when he seen her open her eyes. "Yes, I slept good Daddy. And you might be right. I guess we been holed up in here long enough." Misty replied.

Before they got out of bed Misty looked at Lil Giz and said, "Daddy, I really appreciate you taking care of me through all of this. I don't know what I woulda done witout you." Misty said. "You ain't never gotta worry bout what you gon do wit out me Mama." Lil Giz replied.

"BAM BAM BOOM.....POLICE! GET DOWN! GET DOWN! RANDY JAMES MICHAELS YOU'RE UNDER ARREST FOR THE OAKLAND MURDER OF QUINTIN JACOBS. YOU HAVE THE RIGHT TO REMAIN SILENT........."

"Misty, call ma brother, get a lawyer, and don't

talk ta nobody but them." Lil Giz said as they were

walking him out the door in handcuffs..................

To be continued…….

Keep an eye out for my next series

"Mowgai" that will bring you into the life and

mind of a Gangsta who attempted to change his

life by becoming a Pimp. In the end, it was in em

not on em, the Gangsta that is.

Page 464 of 466